CW01457152

OASIS

ZONE CYBORGS BOOK 3

JESSICA MARTING

SHADOW PRESS

OASIS

Oasis (Zone Cyborgs #3)

ISBN 978-1-989780-16-9

Copyright © 2019, 2022 J.L. Turner

Cover design by German Creative

All rights reserved. This ebook or any portion thereof may not be reproduced or used in any manner whatsoever without the express written permission of the publisher except for the use of brief quotations in a book review.

This book is a work of fiction. Names, characters, places, and incidents are products of the author's imagination. Any resemblance to actual events, locales, or persons, living or dead, is entirely coincidental.

CONTENT WARNING:

This book contains discussion of trauma, abuse, drug use, addiction, and recovery.

For David

CHAPTER 1

VALENNA MERCHANT KEPT her head down, avoiding eye contact and discouraging small talk from her apartment block's other residents. Or maybe they were just strolling in with the rest of the crush of people flowing into the lobby from the street, looking for an unlocked apartment to rob. Or a locked apartment with no one nearby to watch the lock being descrambled. God knew she'd done that, once upon a time.

But not anymore. She'd made it fourteen whole months sober, and sober people didn't have to break into apartments to support their darfin habits. Although it wasn't like she making bank being a law-abiding citizen. That was what she got for staying in Center City, Echo-7's notoriously overcrowded capital. But she hadn't saved up enough scrip to leave yet, not that she was sure where she would go.

I've made it this long sober. I can keep it up.

But even as she silently repeated that pep talk in her mind as she unlocked her apartment door, she was unsure if that was true. Now that the reality of her new life had fully sunk in— her sister, Cressida, still didn't fully trust her, but Valenna was working on that—she didn't know if she could maintain sobriety as long as she stayed in Center City.

She'd cut ties with everyone in her old life. She'd moved across the city, taking over the lease of her sister's old apartment when she moved into a bigger place with her boyfriend, but it wasn't enough.

"Valenna."

Her hand froze over the lock pad.

She'd cut ties with almost everyone, or thought she had. Not that Janek Dalton couldn't track her down if he really wanted to.

She turned around to face the bounty hunter she'd hired over a year ago to look for her sister. "Hi," she said.

"Good to see you. I heard you got sober."

Valenna didn't want to spend any time on small talk with him. "I paid you everything I owed over a year ago," she said.

"I'm not here about that," Dalton said. "I heard you're in some trouble of the financial sort, and I may be able to help you."

She shook her head. "No way." The palm lock whirred, and its indicator light glowed green, but she didn't open the door, not wanting to encourage Dalton to stay any longer. Not that a cheap apartment's basic palm lock would keep him out if he really wanted to get in.

"You don't even know what I have to tell you."

"I'm sure it'll be awful." She crossed her arms over her chest, waiting for him to take the hint and leave.

"It won't be. Three-month assignment on Oh-Three-Oh. Are you familiar with it?"

Valenna racked her brain and came up blank.

"Omega-Three-Omega," Dalton replied. "Way out past the Rims, right on the Brava System border."

"The war's officially over," Valenna said, half to herself. It took over a decade of fighting on and off, but the war between the Zone and Brava System had finally ended less than a month ago. Trade was scheduled to resume for the first time in years; there was talk that the years-long recession on Echo-7 was about to end.

"Yeah, but this job isn't related to peacetime," Dalton said. "You'd be a caretaker of sorts. A housekeeper. Cleaning up, that kind of thing. But it's a remote planet, and there isn't much in the way of neighbors or amusement." His mouth quirked in a smirk, and Valenna wanted to slap it off him. "Or darfin."

She shook her head. "I'm getting by here." And she was slowly repairing her relationship with her sister.

"You're sweeping streets here and the pay's shit," Dalton said. "You could get a lot more on Oh-Three-Oh. More than enough to leave Center City if you want."

He had her there. She didn't ask how he knew she was a street sweeper, a job obsolete on every other planet in the Zone that wasn't so overpopulated that an autonomous cleaning vehicle would be dangerous. "How much?"

Dalton named a figure that had her head spinning. It was more money than she could earn in two years cleaning filthy streets in Center City, or anywhere on Echo-7.

There was just one more thing to consider. "How do you know about this job?" she asked suspiciously. The bounty hunter didn't exactly work within the confines of the law. "And why did you think of me?"

"I have contacts in every area of business in the Zone," Dalton said. "This job popped up on a freelancer's network on the galactic net. And I know that you're still in debt to some dangerous people. Just because you're sober doesn't mean the darfin dealers don't expect to be paid."

God damn it, he had her there. "They sent you to find me."

"And they wanted me to rough you up a little, but I like

you, so I'm offering you an out instead. Your tip with the AWOL cyborg last year really solidified my standing in my community, even if the bounty was shit."

Valenna cringed. "The AWOL cyborg" was her sister's boyfriend, and she didn't think Lukas would ever warm up to her thanks to her involvement in his capture.

She looked away, not wanting to see Dalton gloat because he knew she didn't have much of a choice. She still owed money to unsavory people, and she supposed she'd been running on borrowed time until now.

"Fuck," she muttered.

"I take it you're up for the job," Dalton said. He gestured to the door. "You might want to pack and hustle out of there. I was supposed to send a holo of you with two black eyes to someone about ten minutes ago, and now that I'm past the deadline, another goon is on his way."

Less than two hours later, Valenna was aboard a converted freighter, all of her meager worldly possessions crammed in a duffel at her feet. There were a couple of other passengers who looked just as forlorn and frightened as she felt, but none of them talked to each other. She strapped herself against a bulkhead and wondered just who the captain had to bribe to ensure his ship was certified spaceworthy. Or maybe he hadn't needed to do that at all. It wasn't like anyone important cared about what happened on Echo-7.

She dashed off a quick message to Cressida, telling her she was taking a job on Omega-Three-Omega for a few months and would be in touch when she could. She stuffed the device back into her duffel, not bothering to wait for a reply or even sure if she wanted one. If anything, Cressida and Lukas would probably be relieved to be rid of her for a while.

I can use some of the money to pay back what I've taken. Valenna squeezed her eyes shut as the hazy memories of breaking into her sister's apartment to steal stuff to pawn ran through her head again. The very apartment Cressida had generously signed over the lease after Valenna finished her latest and most successful attempt at rehab.

And after that, I'll be able to leave Echo-7. She thought about buying a cabin on one of the Rim Worlds, far enough away from the darfin sources and bad memories but still in galactic net range.

A cabin, maybe with a pet or two. Just me and the animals. I'll get a job on one of the homesteads there. Or maybe I'll buy a small farm and live off the land. Plant a nice vegetable garden. She'd live an uncomplicated life, and all she had to do to make that dream come true was clean a few bathrooms on a backwater planet.

Shut down.

Anders willed his components into submission, but they didn't obey. He couldn't power down or force his conscious state into sleep or even a trance. No, he was forced to feel everything the Oh-Three-Oh bastard who called himself a doctor was determined to put him through. Still, he tried to circumvent his programming and relieve some of the pressure around him.

Shut down.

He closed his eyes and tried to think of something pleasant. A walk in the forest. A meal at a nice restaurant. Visiting with his long-dead sister, Cecily.

He remained rooted to the floor of the massive water tank in Oh-Three-Oh's Oasis, bubbles trailing upward when he breathed in the freezing cold water.

His ability to do so notwithstanding, Anders thought breathing anything but air had to be the worst part of all of this.

"Barris?" The voice intruded on his thoughts, the volume cringe-inducing. If the ability to breathe underwater like a goddamn fish was the worst part of this, his brain being implanted a direct link to the guy who did it was a close second.

"Barris here." Anders's voice sounded far away even to himself.

"You keep losing focus."

God and stars, Anders hated Dr. Jacoby. He knew he was causing Anders to suffer but just didn't care.

"I'm focusing on the cold," Anders said. "Maybe next time you could let me wear a sweater."

There was a pause as Jacoby digested the suggestion. "A sweater would get wet and hinder your swimming ability."

"You won't let me swim, anyway." Swimming might keep him warm, or at least keep his mind off the fucking cold.

"I'll warm up the water later." But Anders knew he wouldn't. He never did. He only made it colder.

"I have some good news for you," Jacoby said. "You're getting a caretaker."

If his eyes hadn't been damn near frozen in place, Anders would have rolled them. "Aren't you my caretaker?"

"No, this is someone else. She'll provide some socialization for you."

Socialization? Like he was an abandoned dog that was scared of people? "You sure about that, Doc?"

There was another pause. "Of course. I arranged it myself. She'll be living here for a few months, providing some housekeeping for you."

She was lured into this, just like me.
That bastard's plotting something.

"What the fuck?" Anders said. The water somewhat muffled the effect. "Are you bringing me some kind of sex slave? Is that what the next step in this fucking experiment is?" Rage welled up in him, and he knew Jacoby would pore over his emotional responses, like he had to look for a reason he might be angry.

"No, of course not. I hired her to be just what I said. This place needs a housekeeper, and she was willing to take the contract." Jacoby's tone told Anders that he thought he was nuts for even suggesting anything untoward to the new housekeeper, if that's what she really was.

Anders didn't believe Jacoby for a minute. Every enhanced instinct Anders possessed told him that this housekeeper was in danger.

Oh-Three-Oh was the last stop on the way to nowhere. The closest point to civilization was the Brava System, and it was still a hell of a long way away. He wondered what lies had been told to the new housekeeper to entice her to come here.

"Let me out," Anders ordered. "I'm done with the water for the day."

"We're not finished yet," Jacoby said.

"I don't care. I want out."

He could think better when his head didn't hurt from the cold water, when he could focus his eyes. He could think of a way to get that housekeeper away from Oh-Three-Oh and back to where she belonged.

"That's not possible yet," Jacoby replied, voice as cold as the water. "Now, please move forward naturally and easily along the tank floor."

Anders could cooperate, or Jacoby would tap into his brain with that damnable minicomp he always kept in his pocket and force him to walk. So, Anders moved, one foot in front of the other, and hoped desperately that the housekeeper's ship would turn back for her home.

CHAPTER 2

HOW SHE'D FALLEN ASLEEP STRAPPED to a bulkhead, Valenna couldn't say, but she did so, at least until someone shook her awake. Blinking against the hold's bright lights, she faced the freighter captain. "Your stop," he said. "Oh-Three-Oh. Get up."

She unsnapped her makeshift safety harness and stood up on stiff legs. "We're here?"

"That's what I said. And I have one more stop to make before I go back to Echo-7. Shift it."

Valenna slung her duffel over her shoulder, cringing a little at the bag's impact on her protesting muscles. "What time is it?"

"Little after one hundred hours. Any more questions?"

His tone said he didn't want to hear them, so she said, "No."

The hold's exterior door was open, revealing the bright lights of a landing pad. Cold air rushed into the hold, bringing a few snowflakes with it, and she wished she had a heavier jacket. A pair of men outfitted in generic green and gray fatigues stood a few meters away, backs ramrod stiff. Aside from the freighter captain, they were the only people she could see.

The freighter captain shoved a crate at one of the men, and she heard glass clink in it. *Bottles? Is that liquor?*

Then he pushed her toward them, and she stopped thinking about the crate. "Follow them," he ordered. When she hesitated, he barked, "Go!"

They had already turned around and we were walking away. Valenna had to jog to keep up with them. Her duffel bounced uncomfortably against her back and shoulder and her flimsy boots were no match for the snowy ground. "Am I signing any contracts?" she asked. "What exactly am I doing for the next few months?"

Neither of them replied. The freighter's engines rumbled behind them as it prepared for take-off, making conversation impossible anyway.

The only illumination other than the landing pad's lights came from a small, fortress-like structure that looked to be about a kilometer away. If it wasn't for the lack of foliage, Valenna might have thought she'd ended up back on Haven, a planet with an abandoned military installation. She'd been there once and didn't remember too much of it thanks to darfin, but she remembered how bleak and empty its landscape looked even with its sad shrubbery and trees.

"Look, I asked a question," Valenna said. "I'd appreciate it if you could tell me a little about what this job is."

Her only answer from them was silence.

At least it's military. That had to mean a certain level of safety.

But their uniforms aren't military regulation. They were green and gray instead of Zone black.

Oh, God, I'm an idiot.

They approached the fortress and a soldier stepped up to a biometric lock outside a massive door. It cycled open with a near-silent hiss, and they walked inside. A middle-aged man with greying hair clipped close to his scalp waited, a grey lab coat over his dark trousers and shirt. He held out his hand to Valenna in greeting. "Thank you for arriving on such short notice," he said. "I'm Dr. Garrett Jacoby."

She shook it tentatively. "Valenna Merchant. I guess you know Janek Dalton."

Dr. Jacoby let go of her hand. His brow furrowed at her question. "Who?"

"The guy who told me about the job. I guess you weren't able to go through the normal channels to get someone here." She was babbling, a trait she'd noticed she picked up since she got sober.

"Oh, yes," Dr. Jacoby replied, as though Valenna had reminded him of that fact. Her unease grew a little more. "Dalton. He responded to my ad right away. Come with me." To the soldiers, he said, "Take her bag to her barracks and leave us."

Before she could protest, they whisked her duffel off her back, and the soldiers disappeared with it and the crate the freighter captain delivered. Not knowing what else to do, she followed Dr. Jacoby.

"I run a research facility here," the doctor said as they walked through a corridor lined with closed doors. "I'll have you sign a non-disclosure agreement and then we'll tour the facilities. I think you'll find this is a straightforward job for you, but I'm conducting some top-secret research here."

"I doubt I'll see much secret stuff while I'm cleaning the bathrooms," Valenna said, trying to lighten the mood. It was more for her benefit than his.

Jacoby raised an eyebrow at her as they walked but didn't respond.

"That's what caretaking and housekeeping is, right? It's within my skill set." She thought of the amount of money waiting for her if she finished this assignment, more than she could ever earn cleaning Center City's streets. "I don't know if Dalton told you, but I only have my year nine completed." She'd discovered darfin after that and hadn't set foot in a classroom since she was fifteen.

"That won't be an issue." Jacoby pressed his hand against a palm lock outside one of the doors, and it cycled open. "But you will see some things we're keeping under wraps for the time being."

They stepped into an office, where Dr. Jacoby sat down behind a desk. He produced a thincomp from a drawer and handed it to Valenna. "Take a seat, read this over, and sign it."

Valenna sat down on the other side of the desk and accepted the thincomp. Splashed across its screen was a contract, and her distrust of her new home increased as she read through its terms.

"This says if I refuse to sign, I'll have to live outside until the next passenger shuttle comes here," she said.

"That's right. Ships usually only show up for supply drops, and not all of them are willing to take extra people back with them. You're the first one to arrive on one in, well, ever." He gave her a knowing look.

She was trapped here if she said no. *Dalton, what did you get me into?*

She corrected herself. *What did I get myself into?*

Valenna read the rest of the contract, most of which related to her remaining silent about her time on Omega-Three-Omega and everything she would see, along with a clause stating that any of her personal communication devices would be removed from her possession during her time on the planet.

My thincomp's in my duffel.

As if he could read her mind, Dr. Jacoby said, "Your

luggage will be sorted through and any inappropriate devices confiscated."

She hadn't checked it to see if Cressida had replied to her last message. "What if there's an emergency?" she asked.

"We're equipped to handle any emergencies here."

Her unease morphed into outright fear, and as she finished reading the contract, she realized she'd made a huge mistake.

Her hand poised over the device's thumbprint reader. If she signed this, she would cut herself off from the rest of the galaxy for months while she cleaned God knew what in this base.

If she didn't, she'd be turned outside, into Oh-Three-Oh's frozen landscape. She wouldn't last two days out there.

If she did, she could make her money and fuck off when the job was done, and she could have her little house on a Rim World or even the Brava System, far away from Echo-7 and the darfin dealers.

Mistake or not, she couldn't back out now if she wanted to stay alive. She pressed her thumb to the reader, signing the contract, and handed the thincomp back to Dr. Jacoby.

"Excellent," he said. "Now, let me show you the facilities."

"You'll be doing basic maintenance," Dr. Jacoby said as they walked through the corridors. "It doesn't get too bad here, but there isn't enough staff to allocate to cleaning duties. You'll have downtime as well, although there isn't much for you to do here. There are some games and books in the lounge if you want to amuse yourself."

Valenna nodded.

"The soldiers share their barracks and keep it clean, so you don't have to worry about that. You'll be responsible for bathrooms, the shower room, and common areas." They stopped at the end of a grey-walled corridor, and it whirred open for Dr. Jacoby. "I call this room the Oasis. And you'll be helping to look after this fellow."

The room they walked into was large and even colder than the rest of the base. But all of that was forgotten when Valenna saw the massive water tank dominating the room, its plastiglas sides reminding her of a giant aquarium.

And pacing the floor of it, a man facing away from her, hair gently flowing with the water, bare muscled arms held out against his body. He didn't wear any breathing or diving equipment, just a green sleeveless shirt, trousers, and black boots.

"What the hell?" Valenna's voice echoed through the room.

"That's one of my top-secret projects," Dr. Jacoby said with a touch of pride. "And he's part of your responsibilities." A mocking undertone seeped into his voice with his next words. "He's in need of a friend."

"What?" She moved closer to the tank and had to resist the impulse to tap on the plastiglas to get his attention. "How is he breathing?"

"He's been enhanced to breathe underwater," Dr. Jacoby said. "Being able to do such a thing would revolutionize warfare and even has industrial uses. He's responded very well to treatment."

Enhanced. Valenna knew what that was code for. "He's a cyborg."

"If that's what you want to call him, yes," said Dr. Jacoby. "Although the cyborg program was officially discontinued."

Valenna held her breath, mulling this over. Dr. Jacoby didn't know she was acquainted with the only known cyborg in the Zone, that her sister's boyfriend was none other than Lukas Best, the *enhanced* son of a military admiral.

What had she gotten myself into? What had the enhanced

man pacing the floor of a gigantic water tank gotten himself into?

She stepped forward and raised her hand to touch the tank's plastiglas. "Don't touch that!" Jacoby said sharply.

Valenna pulled away. "Sorry," she mumbled.

At that moment, he looked up and caught her eye, starting a bit when he spotted her.

He looked so *sad*.

"Hi," she said, and waved.

Her voice carried vibrations across through the tank's plastiglas sides, through the water, and Anders felt it, as distinct as a warm fingertip across his skin. He remained rooted to the spot, staring at her.

Run away! Get away from here as fast as you can!

But she smiled, and he forgot all about the warnings she needed to hear and heed.

Jacoby appeared beside her, and his surprise evaporated at the sight of the man's punchable face. "That's Barris," he said. Louder, he said, "Barris, this is Valenna. I told you about her."

Anders nodded, then turned his gaze back to Valenna and tried to decipher the look on her face. Surprise and sympathy.

He might have an ally in her. He waved back.

"Time to get out, Barris," said Jacoby.

He walked along the bottom until he reached the tank's ladder, which had been temporarily de-electrified for his use, and scaled it. Dripping wet on the tank's deck, he was colder out of the water than in it, but he couldn't shiver.

But at least he could breathe proper air now. His ocular enhancements sharpened, and they assessed the woman standing on the ground, three meters below the tank's deck: humanoid woman, approximately twenty-four years of age, body temperature a little low on account of the perpetual chill in the Oasis. *She* was certainly shivering.

"Barris, come down." Jacoby's voice broke his train of thought.

Anders could move of his own accord at the moment, but he knew if he delayed obeying the order that he would strip the ability from him. He gripped the deck ladder's cold metal and descended it until he reached the floor. He faced Jacoby and the housekeeper, water pooling at his booted feet.

"You're a cyborg." Valenna's voice was quiet, but he heard the shock in it.

Keeping his expression neutral, he nodded.

"Cyborgs don't officially exist," said Jacoby.

She bobbed her head. "Right." But she sounded unconvinced. The notion that Anders might have an ally in her solidified with that word.

"Barris will take you to your barracks," Jacoby said.

"I'm getting permission to leave the Oasis?" Anders asked. His voice was a rough croak from his time in the water.

Jacoby gave him a sharp look, one that told him to be obedient or else. "Her barracks are next to your accommodations," he said.

"That's what you're calling that broom closet?"

"Barris." Jacoby's voice took on a threatening note, and Anders shut up.

If this wasn't Oh-Three-Oh, and he wasn't a cyborg dripping freezing water everywhere, Anders would have offered Valenna his arm like a gentleman. But it was Oh-Three-Oh, and he was a cyborg, so he said to her, "Follow me."

CHAPTER 3

THE CYBORG DIDN'T RUSH Valenna along like the soldiers and Dr. Jacoby did, which she appreciated. She followed him through the huge room with the tank, down yet another corridor, to a barracks-style room filled with empty bunks, her duffel in the middle of it. "This place keeps getting weirder," she muttered to herself.

"I say that all the time," the cyborg said.

She looked around the room, just to make sure Dr. Jacoby was gone. "Am I going to die here?" she whispered.

"I doubt it."

"I can't believe I took this job." She opened her duffel, and as she'd suspected, her thincomp was gone. The rest of her belongings were raked over, too: the small magnetic box she used to hold her few pieces of costume jewelry was wrenched open, the hinges damaged, and the pockets of every pair of threadbare pants turned inside out.

"Neither can I. What were you thinking?"

"I need the money," she said. "Why are you here?"

"I needed money, too."

She stilled. "Were you ever paid?" *Oh, God, I'm going to*

end up a cyborg or have my organs harvested. Thanks a lot, Dalton.

"You mean, was I lured here with the promise of a job and forced to stay? No." The cyborg's eyes took on a faraway look, and she had the feeling he wasn't with her right then. "I was enlisted," he said. "Jacoby needed paid volunteers for an experiment, and I volunteered." He paused. "My sister needed the money."

But before Valenna could ask him any more questions, he clammed up. "I'll let you get settled," he said. "You might want to take a nap before you start your job."

With those words, Valenna finally realized just how tired she was, and she wondered about the time. It had been after one in the morning when she arrived, and she had no idea how much time had elapsed since then.

"Good night," the cyborg said. He started to walk away.

"Good night, Mr. Barris." *He's a soldier, idiot. Not a mister.* "Sorry, uh, Lieutenant Barris? Captain Barris?"

He turned around to face her. "You can call me Anders."

For the first time in years, Anders didn't mind the cold as much, and the cause of it was the woman living in the barracks next to his room. More of a closet, he thought ruefully as he let himself in. There was room for a narrow bed, a sink, and not much else, not that he had many possessions anymore.

It was a short conversation, but he'd still had one, and Valenna hadn't looked at him like he was a freak or something not quite human. Not that he *was* fully human, but it was still nice to be treated as such.

And he'd shut down when she asked him why he was here. He would've told her about his sister, Cecily, but it was already late for her, and he didn't want to use up all of his conversation topics so soon. It wasn't like they could sit down over beers and talk about their favorite vids or music.

It was the smile that she'd given him when he was still in the tank that had done it for him. His humanity wasn't so far gone that he couldn't recognize friendliness, even if it had been years since he'd experienced it.

He breathed deeply, not wanting to get himself worked up in case Jacoby was monitoring his emotional responses elsewhere on the base. The last thing he wanted was Jacoby in his face, conducting one of his interrogations. They hurt, even for a cyborg, and it had been over a year since the last one. Jacoby had probably dreamed up newer and worse ways to torture him since then.

He stripped out of his wet clothes and dried off with a threadbare towel, then changed into equally decrepit clothes to sleep. It wasn't warm enough in here; it never was. Unfortunately for Valenna in the barracks, it would be freezing for her, too.

He lay down on the too-small bed and closed his eyes, willing himself to get some sleep. He was pleasantly surprised to discover that he was in charge of his enhancements again, and he could power down enough to fall asleep. Part of him thought that might mean something terrible was in store for him the next day and Jacoby needed him alert; another part was relieved that he could get some rest.

But as he nodded off, he thought he might actually dream tonight, and his dreams would feature the new housekeeper.

Valenna awoke, stiff and cold, and marginally refreshed a few hours later when the barracks lights cycled on. Without her thincomp, she didn't know what time it was, and she pawned her mother's chronometer for drug money years ago. The memory of the sale haunted her as she dressed and dragged a comb through her hair, tying it back in a ponytail.

She didn't know what she was supposed to do today, or where she was supposed to report. The barracks door cycled open when she approached it, and she chose the direction she took with Anders, hoping she'd run into someone who could tell her where her mop and bucket would be.

Or breakfast. Her stomach growled, reminding her she hadn't eaten since her lunch break during her last shift street sweeping. One of the long-term effects of darfin use was a decreased appetite, and Valenna had found she wasn't very good at remembering to eat since she got sober. She passed out once from lack of food while she was still at rehab.

She needed breakfast and a mop bucket, stat. Maybe some tea, if they have had it here.

She kept on walking through the maze of gray-walled corridors, hoping she would pick up the scent of food or a soldier or Dr. Jacoby, *anyone*.

Shouldn't a military installation have lots of soldiers?

Valenna stopped dead in her tracks.

This place was huge and was conducting top-secret cyborg research. Shouldn't there be lots of people guarding it?

Shouldn't she have been escorted here by military transport? Why would the military ask bounty hunters to find them a housekeeper?

While Valenna had spent a significant chunk of her life high and ignorant of major galactic events, she wasn't naive enough not to know about the rampant corruption in the Zone. It was, as far as she knew, one of the reasons war broke out between them and the Brava System: the Zone kept trying to annex Brava territory. There were lots of off-the-books projects quietly sponsored by the military with the government's blessing, and Lukas was one of them.

So was Anders, apparently.

"I've made a terrible mistake," she whispered. She almost wished she'd let Dalton punch her in the face to send that holo to whoever wanted to see her beaten.

"Good morning."

Valenna shrieked and turned around to face Dr. Jacoby. Had he heard her muttering to herself? She searched his face, but she saw only a friendly expression there.

"Hi," she said, placing her hand over her rapidly beating heart. "Sorry." She forced out a small laugh, not wanting to give away her fear. "I'm a little lost, and I don't know what I'm supposed to be doing today." Her stomach growled. "And I don't know where I should get some food. That wasn't on the tour last night."

"Come with me. I'll take you to the mess hall."

Valenna followed him and again looked around the featureless gray walls, trying to pinpoint landmarks that would help her get around a little easier. There were none, but she counted the turns they made until they arrived at a large cafeteria-style dining hall.

A group of soldiers sat opposite one another at a long table. She counted six of them, all dressed in the same gray and green fatigues. Six men in a room that could seat dozens. Her unease reared itself again.

"Help yourself to the replicator and processor," Dr. Jacoby said. "I'll be back in half an hour." He walked away from the mess.

Well, that was weird. But then, all of it was.

Avoiding eye contact with the soldiers, she went to the nearest replicator and tabbed in an order for tea, then a ready-meal from the processor. She took a seat at the furthest edge of the table, putting nearly two meters between her and the nearest soldier.

Where was Anders? She looked down the row of faces but didn't see him.

None of them talked to her or each other, but she got a few curious looks. Finally, she decided to break the ice and try to bring a little normalcy to the meal. "Hi," she said. "I'm the new housekeeper."

Dead silence greeted her, save for the occasional sip of coffee.

"I'm Valenna," she tried again. She took a bite of reheated potato mush and barely tasted it.

"Does Anders not eat with you guys?" she asked.

No one answered.

She sighed and turned back to her breakfast. It didn't taste great, but food rarely did for her these days. She wondered if she'd ever like food again or if eating would just be one more bodily function to deal with.

She forced herself to finish the entire ready-meal. She helped herself to another cup of coffee and waited for Dr. Jacoby. She resisted the urge to pace the room to take her mind off of what she'd gotten herself into.

Was Cressida worried about her? Maybe, since she'd been open to repairing their relationship since she completed rehab. Her sister was the only person in her life Valenna was remotely close to, and they weren't that close yet.

Would she worry that Valenna hadn't gotten in touch with her like she promised in her last message? Would Cressida just assume she'd started using darfin again?

The idea brought tears to her eyes. Valenna had been so determined to stay sober, so focused on it, even though it was so hard. *Life* was hard, and earning her living in Center City was nigh on impossible even with the transferred lease from Cressida. It was so much easier when she didn't have any responsibilities.

I have to stop thinking it was easier. It wasn't. My skin was falling off in places where I scratched it too much, I had to scrape and steal to afford the darfin. I would've sold a kidney if I'd kept on using, if Cressida hadn't given me that ultimatum after we got back from Haven.

She discreetly brushed away her tears and hoped none of the soldiers had noticed.

I should've looked up Omega-Three-Omega on the galactic net before I left.

God damn it, she really was failing at being a functional member of society.

True to his word, Dr. Jacoby came to collect her after half an hour had passed. His demeanor was brusquer now, and he shoved a chronometer and scratched thincomp at her. "None of that can connect to the galactic net," he said. "The thincomp has a map of the facility and a list of your duties and schedule while you're here. It's important to follow this."

She brought up the chore list and scanned it. Just as she'd expected, she was required to clean floors and scrub toilets, with some occasional laundry duty thrown in. At first glance, it didn't seem like much, but the accompanying map showed a massive structure to take care of, all on what appeared to be a regimented schedule.

"You're expected to be working from eight hundred to seventeen hundred hours," Dr. Jacoby continued. "I will monitor your work to ensure completion. Fraternizing with the soldiers isn't strictly prohibited, but you'll probably find that they won't want to interact with you that much."

"Mr. Barris seemed pretty friendly last night," Valenna said before she could stop herself.

Dr. Jacoby's brow arched upward, concern across his face. Concern and something else Valenna couldn't identify. "In my defense, you introduced me to him," she hastily added. "He was very nice to me."

"Barris is a special case," Dr. Jacoby said.

"Yeah, I got that when I saw him breathing underwater," Valenna said. "You literally showed me his swimming pool last night and asked him to show me to my room."

Dr. Jacoby blinked. It occurred to Valenna that this had to be the first time in a long time that someone had questioned him. Even though she wasn't questioning his actions and merely pointing them out.

When he still hadn't responded, she added, "He seemed nice, is all."

Dr. Jacoby recovered a little. "Yes, well, I suppose so."

"Am I supposed to avoid him?"

"You won't be able to," Dr. Jacoby said. His eyes narrowed a little, lending him a more sinister look that had Valenna suppressing a shiver. "Of everyone here, I'm sure he'd appreciate your friendship the most. Just remember the terms of your contract and employment. This is still a secret facility, Ms. Merchant, and everything that happens here is classified." His expression shifted back into something less scary, and when he continued, his voice was level as ever. "Now, according to your schedule, you should already be on your way to the laundry facilities."

Valenna knew when she was being dismissed. She looked down at the thincomp, not wanting to meet his gaze and receive the chill there, and walked away.

CHAPTER 4

HE WAS BEING PUNISHED.

It wasn't the first time Jacoby left Anders in the tank for three days at a time, but it was especially irksome since he suspected it was because of the housekeeper. Anders wondered if Jacoby had twisted things up in his mind a little, blamed him for his interaction with her even though the doctor was the one to introduce them. Anders wouldn't put it past him. The man had been even more unhinged lately.

At least the water wasn't quite so cold. It was a comfortable punishment, by Oh-Three-Oh's standards. Or maybe Jacoby had just gone on a short bender since Valenna's arrival. The doctor always made sure to have some liquor delivered periodically.

He slowly paced the bottom of the tank. He'd been in there so long the cold wasn't bothering him as much, or maybe it was because he had something else to think about besides his own discomfort.

Why the fuck does Jacoby want a housekeeper now?

The installation was staffed with cleaning bots. Hiring someone from one of the Zone inner worlds and hauling her here for a few months of washing floors made little sense.

You're a cyborg. You're supposed to be smarter than the average man. Think!

Jacoby wanted her for something else. That had to be it. He'd been too distracted by a new face—a pretty one, albeit tired—and someone new to talk to, who wanted to talk to him, that he hadn't considered the motives behind her summoning.

He kept moving, not wanting to stay still and risk a shock depending on Jacoby's mood, assuming he was even still sober.

Valenna was broke, he could tell as much. She would have been offered an exorbitant amount of money to make it worth her while to end up here. That was the only reason someone would do so.

She obviously didn't have anyone in her life to tell her that signing an employment contract for a job, this close to the border and a war zone, was insanity. No one would miss her if she didn't leave. And the longer Anders stayed here, with communications and access to the galactic net severed, he suspected neither of them was leaving on Jacoby's watch.

What the hell was her deal?

His thoughts were interrupted with a mild electric shock through his boots, and Jacoby's voice flooded his mind.

"I'm going to need you to complete a few running laps around the tank," Jacoby said. Anders felt a familiar rumble beneath his boots, one that told him that if he didn't cooperate, he'd be dealing with a worse punishment than spending a couple of days in the water.

So much for his being on a bender.

Exhaustion and hunger tugged at Anders, but he still moved as best he could. "I think I'd be a better runner if I could get some food into me."

Jacoby was quiet for a few seconds. "You haven't eaten?"

"I've been in here for three days." Anders was careful not to point out that Jacoby was the one to keep him in there.

"Oh." He paused again, and Anders thought he might have actually surprised the doctor. "Well, it seems I forgot about that. We'll save the running test for another day." The water rippled as the tank's floor and ladder were de-electrified. "Take the rest of the day off. You'll be back in here tomorrow morning."

When was the last time Jacoby had forgotten him? For that matter, when was the last time Anders had so much time to himself?

He tried not to smile at the idea of some uninterrupted free time, schooling his face into a stiff expression more appropriate to a cyborg. He half-expected the ladder to still be electrified when he put his hands on it, but nothing happened when he did so. He hauled himself out of the water, the installation's recycled air a cold shock to his skin. There weren't any towels on the deck, of course. Jacoby only offered them if Anders needed to dry off for whatever fresh hell he'd planned.

His clothes squished and dripped water as he walked through the Oasis to his small room. Even his enhancements couldn't keep him from shivering, and the data readout in the lower right of his vision told him the installation's temperature was a couple of degrees cooler than usual.

That fucking sadist.

He grabbed a change of clothes from his room and stalked for the showers. He hated the idea that he'd have to get into the water again, but at least this would be hot, and he wouldn't be submerged in it.

If he ever got out, he was never taking a bath or swimming again. Not that Anders had been much of a swimmer before he landed here. His home world, like most of the Zone's planets, was too filthy to consider swimming in open water.

He shucked off his clothes, the fabric hitting the tiled floors with a squishy slap, and headed for the first shower cubicle in the room. He bypassed the laser cleansing protocol and turned the water function to the hottest as he could stand. It would be short, given that the water supply was limited and perpetually recycled, but it would warm him up a little.

Sufficiently warmed, the tank's chlorine washed off his skin and hair, he stepped out of the cubicle, right in front of Valenna. She wore an oversized base-issue civilian smock and a shocked expression on her face. His sodden clothes fell from her hands.

"I'm so sorry," she said, keeping her eyes on his face. Then she looked away. "I'm just going to, um, wash these." She picked them up again.

"Don't worry about it."

She looked down at her booted feet, suddenly fascinated with the floor. "This is on my list today," she said. "I thought someone left their clothes behind."

Anders reached for the towel he'd left hanging on a peg outside the cubicle and dried himself off, then wrapped it around his waist. "Like I said, don't worry about it. And anyway, nudity's a great icebreaker."

She finally looked up and relaxed a little when she saw he wasn't naked anymore. She still kept her gaze on his face, avoiding looking at the myriad scars mapping his body, places where he was cut into over and over. "You have a good sense of humor for a cyborg," she said.

"You know a lot of cyborgs then?"

"Just one."

He'd been joking, but he could tell she wasn't. He lowered his voice, hoping Jacoby didn't have the shower room under surveillance. He walked toward her until they were nearly nose-to-nose. "What?"

Her pupils dilated, but he knew it was from fear. "I know another cyborg, is all," she said. "When I saw you in the Oasis,

I thought that's why the guy who referred me here told me about this job."

"Keep your voice down," Anders said. "Please."

"Oh, okay," she whispered. "Sorry. God, this place is weird."

"We can talk about the weirdness later," Anders said. "Tell me about this cyborg you know."

"He's my sister's boyfriend. He was in the military. You might've heard of him."

"Possibly, but the Zone military is huge." The last Anders heard, there were over fifteen million soldiers on active duty, many of them sent to die on the border straddling the Zone and Brava System.

"Lukas Best," Valenna said. "His dad was a general or something. He doesn't like me much, so I only know what my sister told me."

Anders didn't need to access his memory banks to recall the name. "Admiral Best," he said. "I know of him. Out of Garshan."

"Do you know Lukas?"

"I know *of* him and that he'd had some enhancements, but that's it." He racked his brain, trying to recall more about the military's only official cyborg success story. Lukas Best would be a little younger than Anders's age of thirty, and Best started the enhancement process when he was a kid.

"Well, he's a cyborg, too," Valenna said. "That's pretty much all I know. But I don't think he can breathe underwater."

"How did he meet your sister? What does she do?"

"She's a contract worker for the Echo-7 public education department," Valenna said. "She's between contracts now."

"So, she isn't military?" Valenna's story just got stranger, but strangeness wasn't exactly out of place somewhere like Oh-Three-Oh.

"No. She ended up stranded on the same planet where he went AWOL. Have you heard of Haven?"

Anders closed his eyes and ignored the ever-present data readout in the corner of his eye. "Yes, I've heard of Haven. That planet was quarantined by the Zone government a few years ago. It's a deathtrap." Its flora and fauna were well-known to be lethal to humanoids.

"Yeah, well, he was living there for a while. Cressida met him and they came back to the Zone, and now they're living happily ever after."

Cyborg status notwithstanding, Lukas Best had to have been a hell of a soldier to have survived on Haven undetected for a period of years.

There was a tinge of something Anders couldn't identify in her voice. Not bitterness or jealousy, but ... sadness? Regret? He sidestepped that, and the urge to ask her how a paper-pusher without any military training hauled a cyborg out of a place like Haven. He could ask her about that later. Maybe she and Cressida had once been close, and Lukas came between them.

She looked away, back at the pile of sodden clothes in her hands. "I should wash these," she mumbled. "Sorry to have walked in on you." She turned around to leave.

"Valenna."

She stopped and faced him again.

He thought about making a pithy remark about nudity but didn't want to freak her out. She was the only woman on a military base, after all. He still didn't know if she would ever get to go home.

"Don't worry about it," he said.

It was easy to avoid everyone on base, Valenna mused as she mopped the floor in the Oasis. The place was huge, and as far as she could see, only eleven people lived there, including her.

It was pointless to be mopping since the tiles were already squeaky-clean and the only people she'd seen in there were Anders and Dr. Jacoby. But it was on the list of things she was supposed to do, and she'd do it.

She reminded herself of the huge payday that awaited her at the end of her contract, and Anders's certainty that she would make it through it. That would make it all worth it.

The empty tank loomed in front of her, its water still and clear. Its plastiglas sides reached up at least four meters, and as she moved around the room with her mop, she spotted a ladder leading up its deck.

How could Anders spend so much of his time in there? What was the point of the experiments?

Did he agree to become a cyborg? From what she'd been able to glean from Cressida, Lukas wasn't terribly thrilled about it.

Guilt plucked at her when she thought of them on Haven, so happy together even though the planet was, in Anders's words, a deathtrap.

She brushed away tears with her hand. Stupid sobriety, making her cry all the time. She'd cried more for her lost parents these last few months than the ten years since they were gone combined. She'd wept for hours when she saw a bird get crushed under a grounded flitter near her apartment. Emotions sucked.

She shook her head, trying to banish any thoughts about her family so she could focus on the task in front of her. *Mop the floor. That's it.*

It was weird that she wasn't supposed to wipe down the tank's plastiglas or ladder. *Show some initiative, Valenna.*

She dug around her cleaning cart for a rag and particle

cleansing powder. She sprayed some on the plastiglas side and touched the rag to it.

A jolt of electricity shot up her arm, wrenching a scream from her. She jerked her hand back so violently that she sprawled out on the wet floor, shaking.

It's fucking electrified!

She stared at the tank, realization settling in.

They're electrocuting Anders. Dr. Jacoby *is electrocuting Anders!*

"What is the meaning of this?"

Speaking of the devil ... Valenna hauled herself to her feet on shaky legs. "Nothing," she said. "Just a mistake."

Dr. Jacoby stalked to the tank, examining the spot streaked with cleanser. "There's nothing on your list that says you're to clean this," he snapped.

"I was trying to be helpful."

"It's electrified."

"Yeah, I know that now." Her burned hand throbbed. She drew the sleeve of her oversized smock over it.

The gesture didn't go unnoticed by Dr. Jacoby. "Let me see." When Valenna hesitated, he added, "I *am* a doctor."

Reluctantly, Valenna held out her hand, palm up, and spread her fingers.

It wasn't that bad, but it was her dominant hand and she would probably be sore for a few days. The burned flesh was deep red but it hadn't blistered, likely because the cleaning rag formed a barrier between her skin and the plastiglas.

Dr. Jacoby's hands were cold as they examined her. "Come on," he said. "Let me treat that in my lab."

Valenna didn't know what was so sinister about the word "lab," but it sent a shiver down her spine that had nothing to do with the Oasis's chill. "I think it's okay," she said, wrenching her hand away. "It'll heal in a day or two."

"I can heal it now. Follow me."

There was something about his tone that brooked no argument. Leaving her cleaning cart behind, Valenna followed him.

Oh, God, what is he going to do to me?

Dalton, if I ever see you again, I'm going to kill you.

Dr. Jacoby's lab was in a large room near the Oasis. Visualizers lined the walls, showing images of most of the base, although she didn't notice one focused on the shower room or her barracks. Maybe Dr. Jacoby granted some privacy there to the troops.

He pointed to a diagnostic bed. "Hop up."

Even though every instinct screamed at her to get the hell away, she did so.

"Lay down."

"Do I really need to be laying down for a small burn?" Valenna asked.

"This wouldn't have been necessary if you'd stuck to your instructions." Dr. Jacoby raised an eyebrow. "You *do* remember your contract states that you're to follow your directions if you want to be paid, don't you?"

Valenna obeyed and brought to her mind a vision of the house she would buy, the garden she'd plant. The new friends she'd make on a planet where darfin hadn't taken its hold.

Dr. Jacoby activated the bed's diagnostic cover, the equipment familiar. She'd had to have overdoses reversed a few times in seedy Center City clinics, and they all used the clunky, outdated diag covers.

"It's just a burn," she said weakly.

"And it's nothing I can't fix." He turned away long enough to poke through a cabinet, unlocked with his thumbprint. He selected an unmarked dermospray. "This'll be of some help."

What the hell was that? "Really, it's fine," Valenna said. "I'll stick to the list from now on."

Dr. Jacoby reached for her burned hand and depressed the spray's nozzle against her skin before she could register another protest. She yelped at the freezing cold sensation. Her hand was unable to move for a horrifying few seconds, then she could clench it into a fist. As she did so, pain radiated up her arm, then disappeared.

"All done," Dr. Jacoby said. He removed the diag cover, and Valenna sat up and jumped off the bed. Without looking at the doctor, Valenna rushed out of the room.

"Oh, Miss Merchant? One more thing before you go."

She turned around in the doorway.

"Don't touch the tank again."

CHAPTER 5

ANDERS'S SENSORS picked up the quick shuffling of feet moving through the corridor, the footsteps those of someone smaller and lighter than he was. *Valenna!*

He brightened a little and sat up from his spot on his narrow cot. It would be nice to talk to her again, hopefully, when she wasn't mortified at seeing him naked.

Her barracks door opened and closed. He got up and made the short trip to her barracks, knocking on the door to announce his presence. He hoped Jacoby wasn't watching him do so.

The door opened, revealing a wide-eyed Valenna. "Hi," she said.

"Hi."

She grabbed his hand and hauled him into the barracks. "Well, this is a nice surprise."

His attempt at levity evaporated when she closed the door behind them. "I don't think Dr. Jacoby is keeping this place under surveillance," she said. "At least, I didn't see it on the visualizers in the lab."

"You went to the lab?"

She held out her left hand, its skin pink and shiny from a healing burn. "I touched your tank," she said.

Once upon a time, if someone said those words to him, he would've made them into a ribald joke. But he wasn't that man anymore, and this was Valenna, who did not know what she'd signed up for, and this was the Oasis tank she'd touched. "Oh, no."

"I assume you already know it's electrified."

"Yeah," he intoned. "I've spent a lot of time in there. Jacoby uses shocks to get my attention when he can't be bothered to say hello."

"Holy shit!" she said. "Oh, my God. I had to go to the lab, and he gave me a dermospray, and I don't know what it was, and he wouldn't tell me." She crossed the room to the bed she'd chosen for herself and plunked down on it, burying her face in her hands. "I hate this place. I don't know what's going on, and I get that it's military, but it's just so fucking creepy!" A sniffle escaped her.

The mad doctor had given her a dermospray against her will? Anders's stomach turned over at the implications.

Anders cautiously moved toward her. "Can I sit down?"

She nodded and moved her hands from her face, now tear-streaked.

He kept his voice down, always uncertain of the extent of the surveillance. "What did it feel like?" he asked.

"Paralysis in my hand, then cold and pain. But it only lasted a few seconds."

"All right." He forced himself to keep his breath and heartbeat steady, not wanting to rouse Dr. Jacoby's suspicions if he decided to remotely monitor his vital signs. "There are a couple of things that could be."

One of which was an anesthetic that would relax her internal organs to more easily allow for major surgery in the coming days, all the easier to add enhancements. But he wouldn't mention that yet, not until he was sure. Jacoby was a coldhearted, masochistic son of a bitch, and Anders wouldn't put it past him to tamper with a healing spray so it would cause more pain.

"Okay," she said. "My hand is getting better, at least."

"That's good. Now, why are you here in the first place?"

"I need the money," she said. "I owe a lot in Center City, and I need it to pay everything back and start my life over. Staying on Echo-7 is a really bad idea for me if I want to keep myself together."

"There have to be better ways to make money."

"There aren't," she said. "Not for me." She looked away for a few seconds, and when her gaze met his again, he saw the shame there. "I needed to get away from Center City."

"Your family's there?"

"Just my sister," she said. She took a deep breath, and he thought she might be on the verge of tears. "And we aren't that close. I wrecked her life on Haven."

Even though his brain had been optimized, he still couldn't make heads or tails of what she was saying. "You wrecked her life on Haven," he said flatly.

She nodded. "Yes."

"Does Haven have an unlimited ice cream shop the Zone isn't aware of? Or a money tree?"

The quip drew a small smile from her. "No."

"Then how the hell do you wreck someone's life there?"

"They were so happy," she said in a small voice. "They had all the privacy they wanted, plus free rent. They made it work with old military rations that were left behind, and I think Lukas had a small garden, too."

"You know that living there wasn't realistic in the long term, don't you?"

"Lukas was there for five or six years, I think."

"Since Lukas is a cyborg, he can withstand the harsh conditions there," Anders said gently. "I doubt your sister could've. Leaving Haven was the best thing for them, as expensive and dirty as the rest of the Zone is."

"No." Valenna shook her head again. "It's more than that. And once I tell you, you're going to hate me, and you're the only person who's been halfway nice to me since I got here."

An odd warmth trickled through Anders at those words. It had been so long since he'd had a friend. This was the longest and most heartfelt conversation he'd had since before he arrived here. The last time he'd spoken with anyone so freely was the last chat he shared with his sister.

But he wasn't here to talk about Cecily. "I doubt that," he said.

"My behavior caused a lot of upset with Cressida," Valenna said. She cleared her throat, steeling herself. "I used to use darfin. Like, a lot."

Anders didn't know if his emotions had been inhibited to such a degree that he couldn't react to that tidbit of information, or if that explanation made the most sense why she was on Oh-Three-Oh. "I see."

"I tracked her down on Haven with a bounty hunter, the same guy who told me about this job," Valenna said. "I robbed her a couple times, too, and when she and Lukas were brought back to the Zone, she cut me off. It took another couple of months after that happened, but I went to rehab. I missed her. She's my only family."

"Valenna ..."

She cut him off. "I owe money to my former dealers. Cressida, too, from over the years. And I've made it just past a year sober, and I can't stay in Center City if I'm going to keep that up. I have to leave. I was thinking about a small place on one of the Rims or even the Brava System."

The Brava System... "Are you nuts?" Anders asked. "We're at war with them."

She gave him a look that echoed his feelings about her sanity. "No, we aren't."

"Oh, sorry. They're still calling it a 'conflict.' And a truce isn't peace."

"The war's been over for months," Valenna said. "Completely over. Troops withdrawn, and the border reopened and all. Zone and Bravan citizens don't even need permits if they want to move between the systems."

Anders stared at her, the data readout in his vision telling him only a few seconds passed even though it felt like an eternity.

The war's over.

He wanted to ask if she was sure, but she hadn't been cut off from the rest of the galaxy for as long as he had been. "It's over," he said slowly. He rose to his feet and paced the barracks.

"Yeah. You didn't know?" There was an edge in her voice, one that had nothing to do with her springing the news of the war's end on him.

"No."

"How long have you been here?"

"Just over four years."

"All of you?"

He nodded. "Well, the other guys came here a little while after I did, but we don't interact at all."

"Oh, my God." Her face paled, and Anders suspected that if she wasn't sitting down, her legs would've given way beneath her. "You don't have any access to the galactic net, do you?"

"No."

"Neither do I," she whispered. "Can't you, I don't know, hack into it? Lukas can."

"I'm an after-market cyborg. I didn't get implanted and whatnot until I landed here."

"Why?" she asked.

"Why, what?"

"Why did you agree to being a cyborg?'

He thought of Cecily. "Like you, my sister was the motivating factor. I was supposed to be paid for agreeing to be turned into a machine, but she died before I got the money."

Her expression softened. "Anders, I'm so sorry."

He could shut off some of his emotional reactions if he wanted to, and he did that now, not wanting to break down when he thought of Cecily. "It was a congenital heart defect," he said before he could stop himself. "We couldn't afford a new heart, organic or cybernetic. The money I should've received from the enhancements would have covered the transplant surgery."

He couldn't keep himself from babbling about Cecily in front of Valenna, but he could and would keep himself from breaking down. "She was the kindest person I knew," he said. "Our parents passed away in an avalanche when we were teenagers, and I raised her as best I could. She was one of those rare people who everyone liked as soon as they met her, and she liked them." Cecily had been incapable of making enemies. Anders remembered the time he told her she should've gone into politics; if anyone could have negotiated peace between the Zone and the Brava System, it would have been her.

"She was twenty-one when she died," Anders continued. "Jacoby told me about her passing himself." The ugly memory of that day, of Jacoby's inability to conceal his gleeful smile as he watched Anders's reaction to the news while he was still stuck in the tank, rose up like one of Haven's poisonous mushrooms sprouted from the ground.

Valenna must have sensed that she'd inadvertently hit a

raw nerve and changed the subject. "How did Jacoby get you here, anyway?"

He was glad for the shift in conversation. "He tracked me down at a medical facility near the border," Anders replied. "I was on a short medical leave for a minor injury. He offered me a bunch of money, I realized I could use that for Cecily's heart transplant, and I came here. I haven't left since." He hadn't even left the building. His world had grown to his tiny closet of a room and the Oasis.

She was quiet for a few seconds. "You didn't get the money," Valenna said, voice flat.

"No."

"I'm not getting paid, either," said Valenna softly, but Anders could tell she wasn't as concerned about her finances right now, that she'd just realized something horrible about Oh-Three-Oh and her role here.

"Probably not."

"They'd never let me leave after seeing you anyway," she said. "There aren't supposed to be any more cyborgs."

"The military and government say a lot of things. If they said they shut down the program or there was only one of them, they're lying. You've lived in the Zone your whole life, right?"

She nodded.

"You haven't figured out yet that we're constantly lied to?"

"I never followed politics," she said bitterly. "Nothing changes much for anyone in Center City, especially if you're a darfin user."

Shame twanged through him at her reaction. She'd just figured out she was trapped on Oh-Three-Oh; she was taking it better than he had. But there was one more bombshell he had to lob at her, and the quicker he did it, the better off she'd be.

"There's probably another reason you're here," Anders said quietly. "A medical one."

Understanding dawned on her face. Her eyes widened in fright, and his ocular sensors picked up her quickened pulse beating in her throat. "He's going to experiment on me." She stood up and began to pace the barracks. "Oh, my God. What did he shoot me up with?"

"Valenna."

"Even when I'm trying my best not to fuck up, I fuck everything up." She scrubbed at her eyes with one of her overlong sleeves. "At least I didn't drag Cressida into this."

"*Valenna.*" His tone was sharper than he'd intended, but it had the desired effect. She stopped pacing and faced him. "Come here."

She did, walking so close to him he could feel her body heat. When was the last time someone was so close to him who didn't intend to inflict pain?

Plus, she smelled good. How the hell did she manage that in this place?

He took her hands in his own and squeezed them. She was so *warm.* "Valenna," he repeated. "I will not let any harm come to you, okay?"

Doubt crossed her face. "How?"

"Please trust me," he said. "The dermospray you got today —it ends there, I promise. Just clean like you're supposed to, follow your instructions exactly, and stay out of Jacoby's way."

His words did nothing to assuage her fear, he could see that. But she nodded. "Okay."

She let go of him to resume her pacing, and the broken contact left him feeling strangely bereft.

It's because she's the first person to touch you in years without trying to hurt you.

It was that, and something else. There was something

about Valenna Merchant that spoke to him, reached him on a deeper level.

"Why doesn't anyone speak?" she asked softly, and he suspected the question was more to herself than him.

"What do you mean?"

"None of the other soldiers talk," she said. "Not to each other, not to me, not to Jacoby. Do they talk to you?"

Anders had to consider that for a few seconds. The only person who ever spoke to him these days was Jacoby. But during his brief encounters with the other grunts, they hadn't spoken then, either. He assumed it was orders from Jacoby.

"No," he said slowly. "But I never thought about it. I don't know them or even their names."

"You don't eat with them or exercise with them?"

"Rarely." He thought they were under orders not to speak to him.

"It just seemed weird when they picked me up from the launch pad outside and didn't even say hello, and we had breakfast together before, and they didn't seem to notice I was there. Not even a look."

It was hard to overlook Valenna. She was a little thin, undoubtedly from her hardscrabble life on Echo-7, but she was pretty. More than pretty, if he was honest with himself. It was the first thing he'd noticed about her when she saw him in the Oasis.

And he'd tamped that interest down, not wanting to draw Jacoby's attention.

He almost told her that, but he didn't want to alienate the only possible ally he had in this place. Instead, he said mildly, "It's unusual. We don't see a lot of new faces around here."

"Maybe they *can't* speak," she said.

If his modified heart wasn't controlled by his cybernetic interface, it would have skipped a beat or two. As it was, Valenna's idea still made him gasp.

It made no sense at all, yet it made perfect sense in a place like this.

A group of soldiers lured here under the same false pretenses as him and Valenna, subjected to a few sham medical examinations, and their voices taken away? All of that was entirely within Jacoby's skill set. "How would we even look into that?" he asked in a hoarse whisper.

Jacoby's voice invaded his mind, blanking out any other thoughts for a few seconds. At first, he thought the doctor had picked up on his and Valenna's conversation. "Get back to your room," Jacoby said.

Anders cringed at the volume level. Valenna looked like she was about to speak, but he held up his hand.

"Yeah," Anders said aloud. "I'll be there right away."

A loud click sounded in his head, noisier than usual. Jacoby was pissed off about something, but at least it wasn't that he was talking with Valenna. He would have shocked Anders if that was the case.

To Valenna, he said, "I have to go. Jacoby's orders." He rose and walked to the door.

She ran alongside him to keep up. "Wait. He doesn't have visualizers in here. I saw them all in the lab."

Anders tapped his head. "He can always find out where I am, and he can always punish me from wherever he is on base. I don't want you to end up punished, too."

She bit her lip, a gesture that he shouldn't find adorable and kissable but did.

"Hey," he said. "You will get off this rock, I promise. And not as a cyborg."

She shook her head. "I'm not."

"You are. And you'll get your new start somewhere in the Brava System, as far away from the Zone as you can get."

"But what about you?"

Her concern for him touched his enhanced heart. No one

since Cecily had cared about him. "Don't worry about me," he said.

Before he could stop himself, he reached out and touched an errant strand of dark hair that had come loose from her ponytail. She surprised him when she closed her eyes and leaned into his hand. How long had it been since anyone cared for her, too?

"It'll be okay," he said. He let her go and left the barracks, and returned to his tiny, lonely room.

CHAPTER 6

NOT WANTING to bring any excess punishments to Anders, Valenna avoided him over the next few days. She strictly followed the schedule Jacoby gave her and took her meals in silence, sometimes with the other soldiers, sometimes not. She tried to notice a pattern of when she shared the mess with them, but so far, it seemed random.

She tamped down her loneliness and fear over never leaving Oh-Three-Oh and threw her energy into her job. She kept an eye out for opportunities to investigate what exactly was going on, but she found none.

Above all, she needed to stay out of Dr. Jacoby's notice. Even if she couldn't leave off this rock, she could still try to help Anders. He'd suffered enough.

And he'd done it all for his sister. He'd been a good sibling, far better than Valenna ever had been.

The burns Dr. Jacoby treated had already healed, with nary a scar. The speed with which she'd healed frightened her, but she didn't feel any different otherwise. As far as she could tell, he hadn't injected her with cyborg parts while she slept. Her body still functioned as it always did since she got sober.

Maybe he hadn't done a cyborg thing to her, and he'd just used existing technology to heal her. It wasn't like Valenna's healthcare experiences extended much beyond being treated for accidental overdoses and rehab. If she'd been burned like that in Center City, she would have just wrapped the injury in whatever she had available and soldiered on.

Speaking of soldiers... She spotted a lone one walking along the corridor, straight ahead of where she was mopping the already-clean floor. She gathered her supplies and followed him as discreetly as she could.

She tried to think of the visualizer feeds she'd seen in the lab, grasping at memories of the areas under surveillance. The corridors all looked the same.

She dearly hoped she wasn't about to make another huge mistake.

Valenna caught up to him outside a door marked "Barracks." She touched his sleeve just as he placed his hand in the door's palm lock. "Hey."

He faced her, shock written across his face. It was the only expression she'd ever seen from one of the other soldiers stationed here.

"Hi," said Valenna again, dropping her voice to a whisper. "I know you can understand me."

The soldier looked up and down the deserted corridor, then faced her again. Slowly, he nodded.

"What's going on here?" she asked. "I'm not in the military, but even I know all of *this*," She gestured around the corridor with her hands. "All of this is super fucked-up." She eyed the spot on his uniform where a name patch should be. "What's your name? I'm Valenna."

He shook his head.

"You can tell me," she said.

He hesitated, then mouthed something that looked like

"Jason" to Valenna. His dark eyes did another furtive sweep of the corridor before he pointed to his throat, then made a slashing motion across it with his finger.

A wave of nausea crested over Valenna at his gesture. She had been right in her idea about the other soldiers being silenced.

"*Can* you speak?" she asked. "Like, was your voice box removed, or is it, uh..." She searched for the right word, wanting to be tactful but needing to get her point across. "Disabled?"

He nodded at the last word. He pointed at his shaved head and mouthed the word "program." It took a couple of tries before Valenna understood.

"You're programmed?"

He nodded.

"Are you a cyborg, too?"

He made a noncommittal gesture with his hand, and she got the message. "You're sort of a cyborg."

He nodded again.

"Well, fuck," she said. "Is that really a thing?"

His gaze met hers, and she saw her feelings mirrored in his dark eyes.

"Are all of you like this?" she whispered.

Another nod.

She thought quickly, processing this information. "Okay," she said. "Wow. Thank you for telling me."

He gave her a thumbs-up and a sad smile.

"I need to get back to work," she said. "But I promise I'll try to help you, all right?"

He gave her another smile, but she could tell he didn't believe her.

The soldier unlocked the barracks door with his hand and walked in, the sound of it slamming shut echoing down the corridor. Valenna collected her cleaning cart and rushed away, desperately hoping Dr. Jacoby hadn't spotted their interaction on the visualizers.

The Oasis was the last spot on her checklist for the day, and with a sinking feeling in her stomach, she made her way there.

Valenna had conducted the rest of her useless duties without running into anyone else, and she prayed that meant she wouldn't see Dr. Jacoby today. Aside from her brief interaction with the nameless, voiceless soldier, she hadn't seen another soul.

But there was Anders, slowly pacing the floor of the tank, his short dark hair floating in the water.

She halted and stared at him. He looked like an otherworldly creature, an illustration from one of the books her mother and later Cressida read to her as a child. The lights in the tank's floor lit him up like an angel.

Valenna nearly tapped at the plastiglas to get his attention but stopped herself in time. Instead, she paused near the tank's wall and waited until he looked up before she waved at him.

A smile broke across his face when he saw her, a real one. An unexpected warmth spread through her at the sight, much the way she felt when he touched her hair the last time they spoke.

She waved at him shyly, then turned back to her cleaning cart. She activated an antigrav cleansing cube, and it zipped around the massive room, its pink and blue lasers disinfecting the space with an audible growl.

All she could do was wait for the cube to finish its program. She looked around for a suitable space to sit and found none. Finally, she sat down on the floor in front of the tank and watched Anders pace.

He stopped in front of her and mouthed, "Talk to me."

Valenna tilted her head. "What?"

His mouth formed more words, but she couldn't understand them immediately.

He tried again, more slowly. "I can hear you through the water." He tapped his head in a gesture reminiscent of the soldier she'd spoken to earlier.

Valenna wanted to tell him what she'd found out but didn't dare. She kept her conversation banal. "How was your day?"

He made a swimming motion with his hands, indicating that he had been trapped in there all day.

She got up and walked along the tank with him. "Have you eaten?"

He nodded and mouthed, "Protein cubes."

Well, that sounded disgusting. "You don't get coffee cubes?" she asked lightly.

That drew another smile from him. *Keep him doing that. He needs it*, she told herself.

Well, he also needed to find his way off Oh-Three-Oh, as did the rest of the soldiers imprisoned here.

"Do you get to swim in there at all?"

He shook his head and pointed to his boots, then mouthed something she couldn't decipher at first. "Gravity?" she suggested.

This time he spoke, his voice muffled by the water. "Something like that."

They both stopped and took each other in. Waves gently ruffled his short hair. She almost reached out to touch the plastiglas again but stopped in time, remembering what happened the last time she did that.

She needed to tell him what she'd found out about the soldiers, and she didn't know when they could speak to one another in private again. She racked her brain, trying to think of something mundane to say if only to keep him company, and came up blank.

The cleansing cube growled behind her, and she jumped out of its way. Its lasers touched the plastiglas before the device suddenly jerked away from the tank. It pushed into Valenna, who moved again. "Damn it!"

The cube stuttered in place for a few seconds before it bumped against the tank's plastiglas, then righted itself and directed its lasers against the room's walls.

"How long have you been in there today?" she asked.

Anders held up five fingers.

"Five *hours*? Why?"

He chuckled and mouthed, "That's nothing."

"That's fucked up!"

His expression immediately grew serious, and he shook his head, holding a finger to his lips. She got the message. *Keep the conversation light.*

"When do you think you'll get out today?" she asked.

Instead of answering, he looked up at a point behind her and above her head. She turned around to face Dr. Jacoby, who'd crept up on her, silent as a cat. Or maybe his footsteps were muffled by the cleansing cube's noise.

"Hi," she stuttered. She hoped she hadn't made things worse for Anders.

But he smiled at her, albeit a predatory smile. She suppressed a shiver that had nothing to do with the Oasis's chill temperature and forced herself to remember what Anders and the other soldiers had experienced.

"We were just talking," she said. Her words came out in a rush, and she felt like a little kid again, stumbling into her mother's room and interrupting her as she pressed darfin patches to her skin. If Dr. Jacoby reached out and slapped her upside the head the way her mother used to, it wouldn't surprise her. Instinctively, she braced herself for a smack. "And I'm cleaning," she added, and uselessly pointed to the cube, now crawling up the wall to the unfinished ceiling that stretched at least five meters above their heads.

"That's all right," Dr. Jacoby said. "I'm pleased to see you're friendly with each other."

Valenna hadn't been expecting that. "You are?"

From the tank, Anders said a watery, "Really?"

Dr. Jacoby gave him a dirty look, and Anders resumed his pacing around the tank's floor, leaving them alone. *But not really*, Valenna reminded herself. *Cyborgs can hear anything.*

"How's your hand?" Dr. Jacoby asked.

Valenna pushed back her sleeve and showed him the healed skin. "Just fine." She pasted a smile on her face. "Thanks for helping me out, and I apologize again for messing up."

Dr. Jacoby stared at her, and for a heart-stopping moment, she thought she was about to get in trouble for talking with the other cyborgs. But he looked away from her, back at the tank.

Valenna let go of a breath she hadn't realized she was holding. Maybe she hadn't been found out.

He touched his ear, and Valenna saw he was wearing a tiny comm piece there. "Barris, it's time to get out. Towel off and hit the shower if you want to warm up." To Valenna, he said, "Come with me." He turned around.

She gave a helpless look at Anders, whose expression told her to listen to the doctor. She nodded and went with Dr. Jacoby.

He brought her to the lab, and fear sliced through when she thought about the silenced soldiers and Anders. "Take a seat," he said, pointing to one of the diag tables.

Valenna hoisted herself up. She tried to speak, but nothing came out. She cleared her throat and tried again. "What's wrong?"

"Nothing," replied Dr. Jacoby. "I'm pleased to see you're getting along with Captain Barris."

It took a few seconds for her to realize he was talking about Anders. "I didn't know he was a captain," she said stupidly.

"Once upon a time." The doctor opened a locked cabinet with a sweep of his thumb and removed an unmarked dermospray, larger than the one he'd used to heal her.

"He's been very nice," said Valenna, not taking her eyes off the instrument. "Um, what's that?"

He looked down at it, surprised. Like he hadn't just removed it from a locked cabinet. "Oh, this? It's the follow-up treatment for your burn."

She shook her head. "That won't be necessary. It's just fine." She almost held out her arm to show him, then remembered in time what he probably wanted to do. She drew her overlong sleeves over her wrists and kept them tightly clenched in her lap.

But he set aside the dermospray and plucked a medicorder from his coat pocket. He held it over her head, but she ducked out of the way. "What are you doing?"

Dr. Jacoby looked at the readout. "Huh. You don't have a Porton chip."

Valenna froze, her breath catching in her throat. Porton chips were implanted into darfin users to curb their dependence on the drug. It was the least-difficult and most-expensive way to get sober, and she couldn't afford one when she stopped using. "No," she said.

He knows about the drugs.

"You've been off darfin for a while, right?"

She nodded woodenly. She thought she might be sick.

"We don't have any here, of course," Dr. Jacoby said.

"How did you know?"

"I did a deep background check on you after you arrived," he replied. "You were placed under a drug-related arrest in Center City when you were eighteen. And my medicorder is telling me you still have Revisto in your sodium voltage channels."

Those charges were dropped; Center City's law enforcement didn't see the point in pursuing a case against a teenage user they found passed out on a bench when they could go after dealers. Dr. Jacoby shouldn't have been able to access that information.

What else did he know about her?

"Yeah," she whispered. "I had Revisto patches in rehab to get through the worst of the detox process." Even with the Revisto taking the edge off, detoxing was the worst thing she'd ever done. She wouldn't wish it on her worst enemy.

Nothing on Valenna's person when she arrived indicated that she'd been a darfin user. Either Janek Dalton told him, which was unlikely, since Dalton hadn't known for sure where Valenna was being shipped off to, or...

She mentally replayed his words. *He did the background check* after *I arrived. He has access to the galactic net somewhere here.*

She schooled her features into what she hoped was a neutral expression. "So, I used darfin for a few years," she said. "It's not like that's uncommon on Echo-7."

"Your body still shows signs of the Revisto, but no Porton implant." He leaned back against the med table opposite hers, medicorder in hand, as he waited for her explanation.

"I couldn't afford it," she said. "Plus, there's the

maintenance. It was cheaper to get detoxed, take what I could for counseling, and hope for the best." She'd had four follow-up counseling sessions after her rehab stint ended. They weren't cheap, either. "I came here to make enough money to leave Center City forever and start over somewhere else. I told you that already." Maybe if she kept talking, he would forget to do whatever it was he wanted to do.

"That's admirable," Dr. Jacoby said.

"Thank you." She slid off the bed. "I'm going to get back to work now."

"No."

Dr. Jacoby's tone was sharp, and it had the desired effect. Valenna stopped dead in her tracks and faced him.

"I can make it so you'll never have to worry about darfin cravings again," he said. "Even if you have to go back to Center City, you won't have them."

"I don't really have *cravings*, exactly ..."

That was a lie. She'd stopped waking up in cold sweats, desperate for a darfin patch to take the edge off being alive, and she'd stopped grinding her teeth. But she still missed her makeshift darfin-oriented family. She missed the breaks from reality the drug offered. Sobriety was lonely and difficult.

She could tell from the doctor's expression that he didn't believe her.

"What if I offered you more money if you let me inject this?" he asked, holding up the dermospray.

"My compensation is already more than generous." She tried to move past him, but he blocked her way.

"I can double it."

She shook her head. "No, thank you."

Is there something I can use in here that will knock him out and I can find out where he accesses the galactic net? And the soldiers' controls, while I'm at it

"Are you worried about the grunts living here? About Barris? Did Barris tell you he thinks he's here forever?"

She didn't respond.

"They *want* to be here. They volunteered for it," said Dr. Jacoby. "Protecting a military installation is a lot safer than dodging laser strikes on the Brava border, isn't it?"

"The war's been over for months," said Valenna.

"Yes, but they don't know that," said the doctor. He gave her a hard look. "And I'm sure I can trust you not to say anything."

He doesn't know I told Anders about the war! Despite everything that was happening, a tiny flare of hope rose in her, bright as a flame. If he wasn't keeping her barracks under surveillance for whatever reason, that meant she and Anders had enough privacy to talk strategy for escape.

"No," she said. "Of course not. None of the soldiers besides Captain Barris even speak to me."

Dr. Jacoby didn't elaborate on why that was. "They're focused on their assignments," he said. "And that reminds me of something I need to tell you about Captain Barris."

"He isn't in trouble for talking to me while he was in the tank, is he?"

"No. Quite the opposite, I'm glad you're becoming friends." He cleared his throat and looked away for a few seconds. "And this also relates this to your payment. You still have a uterus."

Valenna stared at him. It took a few seconds for his words to process themselves in her mind. When they did, all she could say was, "What the fuck?"

Dr. Jacoby chuckled like he hadn't just asked the most inappropriate and weirdest question she'd heard in recent times. "You haven't sold your uterus to a needy person to support your former habit." He would already know the answer to that question.

"No." Shock gave way to anger. "Darfin users aren't eligible donors." She'd tried once to sell hers. Healthy reproductive organs fetched handsome prices for their desperate owners in Center City and were often cheaper to the purchasers than cloned ones. "And you know, Doctor, that's a fucked-up thing to ask. This whole setup is kind of fucked." She almost declared that she wanted to go home, but stopped herself in time. She still had to try to save Anders and the others.

She tried again to leave, but Dr. Jacoby grabbed her shoulder and held her in place.

"I'm doing valuable work," he said, voice cool and level. "And I need an infant to continue some of that work."

"What?"

But she knew exactly what he meant.

She thought about Lukas, Cressida's cyborg boyfriend. Hadn't he been a cyborg since he was a kid? Didn't that research already exist?

In that instant, realization hit her with the same force the electrified Oasis did. She wasn't leaving Oh-Three-Oh. She may as well tell Dr. Jacoby what she knew.

"The military already has a cyborg they raised from childhood," she said. "I know him, sort of. Lukas Best."

Her words didn't have the impact that she'd hoped they would. Dr. Jacoby merely blinked and said, "Oh, did he turn up?"

"I—yeah."

"The admiral was too soft on him," said Dr. Jacoby. "And he stood in the way of scientific progress. Some of us are continuing the work that still needs to be done." His mouth thinned. "Will you think about what I said about a baby?"

"You know that I'm probably the last person in the galaxy who should be a parent, don't you?"

"You don't have to parent it, just give birth to it," said Dr. Jacoby, as if that made things better.

"And Captain Barris would be the father." Valenna's words caught in her throat. "You want me to be livestock!"

"You would help to advance cyborg research," he said impatiently.

She shook her head. "No."

His eyes widened in surprise. "Are you sure about that?"

"Yes!" She was finally successful in pushing past him, and before she could stop herself, she said, "I want to go home."

She could help everyone on Oh-Three-Oh from Center City, couldn't she? Wouldn't Lukas want to help his fellow cyborgs? God knew he was smarter than Valenna ever would be.

"What if I told you that if you refuse, I'll have to get someone else? What about Cressida?"

Valenna's blood froze in her veins, and she turned around.

"You couldn't," she said. "Lukas would rip you apart before that happened."

"Maybe he would, maybe he wouldn't. But the threat to her still stands."

Everything Valenna had ever done to Cressida flashed through her mind. She couldn't let *that* happen to her, too.

If she pretended to agree to Dr. Jacoby's insane demands, she could buy herself enough time to formulate an escape plan. "Goddamn it," she said.

Dr. Jacoby smiled. "Just one more thing." He held up the dermospray.

"No," said Valenna sharply. "I'll think about the baby thing, okay? But you don't get to shoot me up with anything more. I still don't know what was in the last one."

"It was just a regular healing treatment."

"And that one?"

He looked down at it. "Preliminary nanobots. They can repair damaged organic tissue."

Oh, my God. "No," she snapped. "Not that, not yet. That's my one condition. Okay?"

He stared at her, eyes narrowing. Even though her legs were shaking from fear, she didn't tear her gaze from his.

"All right," he said. "For now."

CHAPTER 7

ANDERS COULDN'T HELP but shiver on the walk to the shower room, his body much more chilled than usual. Had Jacoby been messing around with the base's environmental controls, or had he secretly adjusted Anders's body's ability to regulate its temperature? He did a quick self-diagnostic but found nothing changed.

Anders took a short shower—noting with some disappointment that Valenna didn't interrupt him—and, not having anywhere else to be, returned to his small room. He found Valenna waiting outside the door for him, and his heart did a happy little flip when he saw her that had nothing to do with his cybernetic organs malfunctioning. "Hi," he said. "What brings you here?"

She barely contained her panic, and his good mood at seeing her evaporated. "All right," she said, voice high. "Um, can we talk? It's important."

"Sure," he said. "I was going to run to the mess for some protein cubes first, if that's okay with you."

"I have food," she said. "And tea cubes, if you want tea." Her voice wavered. "Please. It's important."

Anders recalled her stilted attempt at conversation earlier, and he wondered what she'd found out. "All right."

They made the short trip to her barracks, the room cold and empty of any personal touches save her duffel, open on the floor next to the bottom bunk bed she'd picked out. She picked up a sandwich from a tray on one of the beds and handed it to him. "It's still warm, if you want it," she said. "The sandwiches from the processor in the mess aren't that bad."

He hadn't eaten anything but those stupid, tasteless protein cubes in days, and he accepted it. "Thank you."

"There's more, too. I figured you're burning so many calories trying to stay warm in that water, and—" She paused. "Why the hell are you always in the water, anyway?"

"Beats me. I do it or I get shocked. I don't have a lot of choice in the matter."

"Want some tea?"

"I want you to tell me what's bothering you."

She closed her eyes, collecting herself. "It's a few things," she said, voice a whisper. "But first—can Dr. Jacoby tune into your head?"

"Not my thoughts, no." Jacoby could force him to march on command if he wanted, though. The possibility that the doctor could just kill him and analyze his brain for his memories or knowledge hadn't escaped him, but he wasn't about to freak her out any more telling her that.

Valenna nodded, accepting his explanation. "There are two things I have to tell you," she said. "First, the other soldiers here are cyborgs, too. They can't speak. Dr. Jacoby controls their voices. I found one today, and he signed to me as best as he could when I asked him about why this place is so fucked up."

The other grunts being cyborgs was an insane explanation, but it made the most sense. And while he was confined to the Oasis, at least he could still speak and move of his own accord.

"Do you think you could communicate with them?" Valenna asked.

"You mean sharing a broadcast link?"

"Yeah, I guess."

He considered it. "It's possible," he said. "I'd have to get control over whatever Jacoby's using to speak to me, and I can't do that right now."

"But it's *possible*."

"As far as I know. But keep in mind, I'm a soldier. I know how to shoot things and walk around a cold water tank in the name of research. That's it."

"It's more formal education than I have, so I'll take that." She looked away, and he had a feeling he wouldn't like where the conversation was heading. "There's something else. Dr. Jacoby told me why he brought me here."

Anders nodded, waiting for her to continue.

"He wants us to have a baby," she said after a pause. "He wants to raise it, but I don't think it would live that long."

Anders stared at her, processing that information.

It was monstrous. It violated every ethic he knew a medical practitioner should have, but it wasn't like Jacoby demonstrated much of them. It was exactly the thing a sadistic tyrant like him would do.

"He said he'd pay me more, but I know I'm not leaving here alive," Valenna whispered. "I don't think any of us are. I told him I'd think about it, but of course, we're not going to do it." A humorless, hysterical laugh escaped her. "I don't know about you, but I'd be the worst fucking mother in the galaxy, and I'm including my own mother in that count." She plunked down heavily on her bunk bed. "It's why Dr. Jacoby doesn't care that we talk to each other. He's happy that we're friends."

"Valenna."

"I still have my uterus, even though I tried to sell it a few years ago. I'm pretty sure I can't have kids, anyway. Long-term darfin use permanently scars Fallopian tubes and the uterus. I haven't had a period in a couple of years."

"*Valenna.*"

"I know you probably don't want to hear about that. But he tried to give me nanobots today! Without asking first!" With that pronouncement, she burst into tears.

He sat down next to her. "Valenna," he repeated. "No one will force you into having a kid."

"I'm going to kill Dalton," she said through her tears.

"Who's Dalton?"

"The motherfucker who brought me here," she said. She sniffled. "He must have known something about this wasn't right. He deliberately recruited me to come here." He stared straight ahead, lips in a tight line. "If I have to do it from beyond the grave, I will."

"*When* we get out of here," Anders said. "I'll track him down for you." A resolute strength, the likes of which he thought had been beaten or electrocuted out of him years ago, rose within him. It wasn't just him, a man who was the last of his family, who had nothing to lose except his sad excuse for a life, to consider. Not that he now knew Valenna was in danger, that the other guys here couldn't even talk without Jacoby pressing a button.

"Dr. Jacoby has access to the galactic net," Valenna said. "He told me he did a background check when I got here and accessed my medical and rehab records. He knew about an arrest a few years ago that was supposed to be expunged from the public record. But I don't know where he accesses it. He took my thincomp when I got here, and I don't know where he hid it." She closed her eyes in frustration and pinched the bridge of her nose between two fingers. "Like, I know all these things I'm probably not supposed to, but I can't make sense of any of them to find a way out of here."

Suddenly, she straightened. "There isn't a ship or shuttle anywhere, is there?"

"That would make things easy," said Anders gently. "As far as I know, the only time anyone here deals with a ship is when one drops off supplies."

"Am I the only person Dr. Jacoby's brought in?"

"The only civilian I know of, yeah."

"Okay," she said. Then, more to herself, she added, "At least I'm not the latest housekeeper who will end up dead, tossed in a ditch."

Something inside Anders twisted in anger at the thought of anyone hurting her. Hell, he was ready to tear Jacoby limb from limb for trying to shoot her up with nanobots without permission. Except..."Why would he give you nanobots when you don't have any other cybernetic enhancements?" he mused.

"He said they were preliminary nanobots. Probably to fix my reproductive system."

She was quiet for a moment, thinking. "So, what do we do?" Valenna asked softly. "None of us can stay here, and we can't communicate with the other guys so Jacoby doesn't know."

Anders already had an answer. "That's easy. We'll kill him."

Valenna found herself shocked into silence. She stared at Anders, her brain trying to process his casual suggestion.

And yet ... it may very well be the only thing they could do to save themselves. Even if the doctor wasn't totally unhinged, she knew, deep down, that he would never let any of his science experiments leave Oh-Three-Oh alive.

It's him or us.

"Okay," she said weakly.

"Okay, we kill him? You're okay with that?"

"I don't see another solution," she said. "He's controlling everyone's body here except mine, and I don't know how long that'll last. He's the only doctor here, right?"

Anders nodded. "Someone else used to stop by, but I haven't seen him in months. Military or ex-military, I'm not sure. His name is Byers. He'd watch me in the tank, but that was it."

If this Byers guy hadn't been there for that long, he might well never return. "Do you know how often supply ships come here?" she asked.

"Not exactly. But I'm sure we're due for one soon. Either the base is running low on fuel, which is why it's freezing right now, or Jacoby wants to remind us peons who's in charge. It's been a lot colder than usual lately."

Valenna *was* colder than usual. "It isn't in my head then," she said. She got up and stripped a blanket off another bunk, shaking off its dust. "Want one?"

"You know, I would."

She pulled another blanket from another bed, shook it out, and handed it to him. She took her seat next to him, wrapped in the blanket. "Can you regulate your body temperature? I think Lukas can."

"Yeah, but I miss some regular human comforts, you know? Plus, anyone would get chilly being an aquarium exhibit all day."

Other human comforts that he would have missed while trapped here flashed through her mind, and she felt herself blush. She missed them, too. Long-term darfin abuse had a way of annihilating someone's sex drive until they stopped using.

He noticed her flush. "Everything all right?" He caught himself. "I mean, I know nothing is, but besides being here."

"I can't believe I'm talking about killing someone," she whispered.

"I'll do the actual killing, if that makes you feel better."

She couldn't picture this gentle, kind man doing such a thing, but he *was* a soldier and a cyborg. For all of the terrible things Valenna had done, as far as she knew, her actions had never led to the death of another person. "Is it awful that it does?"

"Considering the circumstances, no."

The enormity of what they could face really hit her, and she felt herself shiver in a way that had nothing to do with the cold. "Wow," she said.

"If there's a way for all of us to escape without killing him, we'll do that," Anders promised her. "But you need to go into this knowing that could happen. I'm not going to let you end up impregnated against your will. And now that I know what's happened to the other soldiers, I won't let them suffer anymore, either. We're in the best position to help them." He hesitated. "Want a hug?"

The question was so unexpected she could have laughed. "Are you serious?" She searched his face, saw only sincerity there.

"Yeah."

"I think I would," she said, echoing his answer about the blanket.

He didn't waste any time draping his blanket around her shoulders. He pulled her close and she leaned against his chest, grateful for the contact. *When was the last time I hugged anyone? Or touched them?*

It pained her to admit that she couldn't remember.

She could hear his heartbeat, a steady, calming sound that sounded normal. "I guess your heart is cybernetic," she said.

"Yeah, but all that means is I'm not supposed to be able to panic during an emergency." His voice was a pleasant rumble.

"Have you ever had a panic attack?" she asked, then immediately felt like an idiot. "Sorry, I know you were in the war. I'm sure it happened."

The war that had been over for months, that he hadn't known about until she told him.

"Yeah, but I wasn't on the front lines like some of the other guys here probably were. Jacoby was looking for a healthy person of the soundest mind possible when he recruited me." He leaned back a little, and she did the same, not wanting their contact to end.

He tightened his hold on her in response. "My sister was dying, and Jacoby offered me enough scrip to save her and get her a new heart. I was supposed to have the cyborg surgeries, let him show me off to some of his friends, and then I'd get the scrip to save Cecily."

"But it didn't happen," Valenna finished for him.

"No. By the time we got to the end of our contract and I was scheduled to go home, he put me in the Oasis. He was the one who told me Cecily died."

She heard the pain and guilt in his voice, that sure knowledge that he'd failed the only family he had left. She'd experienced that too, but not in the altruistic way he had.

"I'm sorry," she said simply.

"Thank you. I still miss her so much, and I've thought about what I could've done instead of this to save her." His voice wavered, but he continued on. "She was one of the nicest people you could imagine. Just one someone who was kind for the sake of being kind, who could make friends anywhere. You would've liked her. Everyone did."

Like Anders was. Valenna could see him coming from a loving family.

They were quiet for a few moments, and Valenna rested her head against his chest, his breathing nearly hypnotic. "When do you have to go back to the tank?" she asked.

She felt him shrug. "Whenever Jacoby orders it."

"Want to stick around here?"

It wasn't a come-on. She couldn't deal with that right now, and she suspected he couldn't, either. But she didn't want to be alone, not knowing what Dr. Jacoby had planned for her.

When he didn't respond, she added, "I mean ... I don't know about you, but I need a friend right now. And if we're spending time together, maybe Dr. Jacoby won't think we're planning to do what we're planning to do."

He rearranged the blankets around them and lay down, fingers entwined with hers. "Yeah."

CHAPTER 8

ANDERS'S internal alarm clock woke him at half-past six, and he tried to get out of bed without disturbing Valenna. It had been nice, albeit cramped, sharing a bunk with her. Like she'd said the night before, it was good to have a friend in times like these, although his feelings toward her weren't strictly friendly.

Messing up their alliance because he had a bit of a crush on her, especially since Jacoby had such horrific intentions in store for her, was the absolute last thing he wanted to do. There was something about her that touched him, reached a part of him he'd kept locked down from the moment he heard Cecily died, and he'd missed that part of himself.

His attempt to leave without disturbing Valenna was in vain, though. She stirred and said sleepily, "You're off already?"

He nodded. "I want to get something to eat before Jacoby makes me do whatever he wants to me to do today."

She leaned on her side, propping herself up on one elbow. "Is there anything he makes you do that *isn't* pacing the tank?"

"Sometimes I have to swim."

"You know what I mean."

Anders gave a half-shrug. "When he started leaving me in there, he said he was trying to find a way for cyborgs to breathe without air. I guess it would be useful in space. I can breathe under water just fine."

Valenna sat up and drew the blankets over herself, still wearing the oversized garments she'd had on the day before to guard against the cold. "I'm not a scientist, but I'm still pretty sure there are other factors to surviving in open space without an EVA suit besides the air thing. Wouldn't your skin peel off in space?"

"If I'm lucky. And don't talk about that in case he hears. I don't want him to get any more ideas."

"I guess not." She glanced at the Jacoby-issued chronometer still strapped to her wrist and her eyes widened. "I need to get up, too." She tossed the blankets off and got out of bed in stocking feet. "And I didn't take a shower last night, so I'll have to do it now. Damn! It's cold." Catching Anders's eye, she quickly added, "Not that I'm complaining. Much."

"You aren't a cyborg. You can complain about the cold. I feel it, too."

She stepped into her boots and collected a change of clothes, and they left the barracks. Anders half-expected to see a gloating Jacoby waiting in the corridor, but there was no one there.

"I guess I'll see you later," Valenna said.

"Yeah."

She looked like she wanted to add something else, but stopped herself in time. The visualizers, Anders remembered. He wondered what Jacoby would say to him today.

She gave him a small wave and took off in the shower room's direction room.

His summons came a few moments later. The data readout in his vision was interrupted with the words, "THE LAB, NOW."

He sighed and said aloud, "I'll be right there."

To get to the lab, he had to walk through the Oasis, where the emergency lights winked and the tank's interior lights were shut off. His heat sensors didn't read an energy signature, which meant the tank would be even colder than usual. He suppressed another sigh and hoped he wouldn't have to hang out in the water today.

Jacoby waited in the lab's doorway, and when they walked into the room, Anders saw the lights were dimmed here, too. He didn't comment on it. "How goes it?" Anders asked, trying to keep his voice light.

"The base isn't out of fuel," Jacoby said, more to himself than Anders. "But it's acting like it is."

He spoke of the installation like it was as sentient as Anders or the other soldier-cyborgs. That he could control it as easily as the grunts here. There was a problem that he couldn't fix, a weakness in the base.

Judging by the stress lines bracketing Jacoby's mouth, the way he kept clenching and unclenching his fists in impotent anger, this wasn't something he experienced that often.

Anders was unsure how to react. "Will the military be of some assistance?" he asked, keeping his voice as steady and reassuring as he could. It reminded him of the times when he was a kid and he'd have to de-escalate Cecily's panic after a nightmare. She'd had a lot of them after their parents died in an avalanche on their home world.

Jacoby's head snapped up. "Of course not."

"But this is their base," Anders said. "They'd want to know if something was wrong with the life support."

"Even if the life support failed, we'd still live," Jacoby snapped. "The air here is perfectly breathable, you know that."

Anders nodded.

He could snap the doctor's neck right now.

He could kill the bastard, and with Valenna and the others, find a way to get off this rock and get back home.

He flexed his fingers, if only to make sure he could still do that, to assure himself that Jacoby wasn't controlling his bodily movements now. He would raise his hands, wrap them around the doctor's neck, and just... twist.

"Did Valenna speak to you?" Jacoby asked. He crossed the room and tapped at a wall-mounted thincomp. Moving yellow dots appeared on the screen, one of them on one side of the screen, the others lumped together in another, unmarked section on the opposite end. It took a few seconds for Anders to recognize the pattern of corridors and rooms. He was looking at a location map of the installation.

"Valenna?" He immediately recalled their conversation from the night before. Despite his cyborg status and Jacoby's appalling desires, he felt himself blush. "Yes, she did."

Jacoby watched the lone yellow dot move away. "What did she say?"

"She told me about the baby thing." Even though he was nearly ready to kill the doctor, Anders asked, "Are you sure about that?"

"You're both reasonably healthy," Jacoby said. "You should both be capable of it. You'll both be compensated for advancing cyborg research."

"I've been waiting for my compensation for years, not that it matters now," Anders said bitterly.

And why not? He would kill Jacoby in the next few moments, anyway.

"Are you referring to your sister? She was going to die, anyway."

Jacoby's flip response resurrected old anger and grief, his words once again piercing Anders's soul in a way he hadn't known possible until he was turned into a cyborg.

"I would've been able to save her if I'd been paid on time!"

Anders roared. "All I was supposed to do here was let you give me a cybernetic heart and lungs, and then I could've paid for Cecily's surgery. But you kept holding it back and making your demands that much worse, and now she's dead. We both know I'm never leaving here, and neither is Valenna. Are you going to turn her cyborg after she has a kid, or are you just going to kill her?"

He lunged, but Jacoby ducked out of the way.

"God *damn* you!" Anders shouted. He grabbed Jacoby's arm, tearing his lab coat's sleeve. Jacoby grabbed something in his pocket and Anders's body immediately froze in place. He crashed to the floor, landing on his face, and felt his nose crunch.

Fuck!

He couldn't force himself to stand up or even move a finger of his own accord. He remained, planted face-first, on the floor.

He saw Jacob's booted feet move away from him. "Are you done?" the doctor asked.

Anders tried to speak but couldn't.

"Never mind answering," Jacoby said. "I was going to have you go outside and conduct some repairs on the exterior fuel line so we'd all stop freezing our asses off, but you're going back to the tank instead."

Anders jerkily pulled himself to his feet. He felt like a marionette. He couldn't fight whatever Jacoby was controlling him with, so he went with it and wished he could check his nose, feel out the damage. His nanobots had already started their repair work, and it was so itchy as to be painful.

He clomped to the lab doorway with all the finesse of a toddler learning to walk. His voice worked again by the time he crossed its threshold, and he said over his shoulder, "Leave Valenna alone."

It was funny, but Valenna had never really noticed the lack of windows until the base's lights started flickering late in the afternoon.

Does Oh-Three-Oh even have its own sun?

She activated a cleansing cube over the darkened, empty mess hall. The only thing the replicators had spat out for her was a protein cube and half a cup of lukewarm, stale-tasting coffee.

It must have a sun. The planet wouldn't be habitable without it.

She hadn't seen sunlight since she left Echo-7.

Well, that's the least-weird thing that's happened to me since I got here.

Valenna left the cleansing cube to do its work and ventured into the corridor. As she did, one by one, its lights turned off. Orange emergency lighting replaced them, but it wasn't bright enough to see clearly.

A chill crawled down her spine that had nothing to do with the base's cold.

"Hello?" she called down the corridor.

Silence greeted her, and if not for the fact that the base was on a habitable planet, she would have worried about suffocating to death after the life support shut off. Lucky her, she would get to freeze to death instead.

She followed the orange lights, most of them flickering, reminding her of flames. "Hello?" she called again. "Anders? Dr. Jacoby?"

She forged on, down a corridor with a single emergency light at its end. "Is anyone there?"

Where were the other soldiers? Had they finally revolted and killed Dr. Jacoby?

"Anyone?" she tried again.

She backtracked from the darkened corridor and took another route, one that would take her to the Oasis. The lighting here was intermittent, and two of them blew out as she walked below them, but she kept moving.

She needed to see Anders, needed to know he was safe. She desperately hoped he wasn't in pain or being punished, but something in her gut told her that wasn't the case. She tried to tell herself she was feeling off because the base seemed to be shutting down, but it was to no avail.

A figure stumbled out of a room off the corridor, and Valenna screamed, the sound bouncing off the walls. It took a few seconds for her to recognize Dr. Jacoby.

"What's going on?" she asked, not bothering to hide the high, terrified notes in her voice.

"It'll get fixed tomorrow," Dr. Jacoby slurred. He tripped, then threw his body weight against the corridor wall. "Damn."

"Are you all right?"

Even in the dim lighting, Valenna could see the contempt on his face. "Of course not."

"Can I help you?" She despised the man, but she still needed to stay on his good side until she figured out a way to escape.

He didn't move from the wall. "You can stop your screaming and act like a goddamn adult."

A memory rushed back, as cold and unwelcome as the base now was. Her mother yelling at her to stop her shrieking and grow up, to leave her alone, the hard slaps she gave Valenna and Cressida for daring to wake her up. Then the cursing as she lurched back into her bedroom, the crying when she realized her darfin supply was depleted.

Valenna remained frozen in place, unsure how to react.

Dr. Jacoby pushed himself off the wall and stood on unsteady legs, directly across from Valenna. "Just—it'll be over soon."

She smelled the alcohol on his breath, the stench overpowering. She recalled the night she arrived, the crate the freighter captain handed to the silent soldiers, the distinct clink of glass bottles inside. She took a tiny step back. "Okay," she said.

"Good." He moved away, leaned against the wall again.

"Where's Captain Barris?" she asked.

"Oh, *him*." But Dr. Jacoby didn't elaborate. "You know, I'm starting to get really pissed off at Byers not getting back to me."

Anders had mentioned that name the night before, but she feigned ignorance, wanting to draw more information from him. "Who's Byers?"

"A colleague with similar aims." His tongue tripped over the words, but he managed to get them out. "Haven't heard from him in months. I'm getting worried."

He didn't seem to want to elaborate on his history with Byers. "Captain Barris," said Valenna urgently. "Where's Anders?"

Dr. Jacoby waved his hand dismissively. Or what he probably thought was dismissively, since he was too drunk to make the gesture effective. "I altered a few of his functions until he can stop being a fucking spoiled brat, but he's in the Oasis if you're looking for him."

"I am," she said. "Thank you."

"He's being a prick about what we discussed yesterday," Dr. Jacoby added. "I'd appreciate it if you worked on that with him."

Oh, God, what had the doctor *done*? Trying to keep her voice calm, Valenna said, "I will." She paused. "Um, how do I get him out of the tank if it's electrified?" She could hardly help Anders if she was burned again or worse.

Dr. Jacoby patted his lab coat pockets, and she saw now in the dim light that the coat was torn. He pulled something out from one, a small device she couldn't see clearly, and pressed his thumb against it. "I'm locked in here," he said, pointing his thumb behind him. "I'm armed. Tell him to leave me the hell alone."

Frustration welled in her at his not answering her question about the tank's electrification. "I'll do that."

She left Dr. Jacoby against the wall and took off for the Oasis.

Anders sat on the tank floor, grateful his limbs could now move of their own volition, and leaned against the tank wall. He drew up his legs and wrapped his arms around them, trying and failing to get warm. He didn't need his sensors and visual data readout to tell him the water's temperature was rapidly dropping.

He couldn't get warm, and while he could move, his body was too frozen to swim. Even breathing had become difficult, and he wondered if his ability to do so underwater was failing. His nose hadn't healed yet, which meant his nanobots weren't functioning as they should. He was finally falling apart.

He thought of Cecily, the guilt he would always harbor over her death. Then he thought of Valenna, how she was tricked into coming to Oh-Three-Oh, and was still alive.

He gritted his teeth and tried to force himself to his feet, which he could hardly feel.

Anders wasn't the only thing failing, it was the entire base.

He heard tapping at the plastiglas wall, a few meters from where he was struggling to his feet, and focused on it. It took a few seconds for him to make out Valenna's form. "Don't touch the walls," he tried to say, but his face was frozen, and the words came out garbled.

"It's okay," she said, her voice sounding far away. "It's been de-electrified. How do I get you out?"

What the actual fuck?

"Dr. Jacoby is falling-down drunk," she continued. "Where are you? The emergency lighting's mostly out in here."

Was it? He squinted in the darkness. He blinked, trying to switch his ocular functions to night vision.

"Whoa," said Valenna, and she sounded closer. "Your eyes are glowing."

She was right in front of him now, and he pressed a hand to the plastiglas in a futile attempt to get closer to her. She did likewise, and he thought he could feel himself thaw out a little.

His data readout told him the water's temperature had dropped another degree and a half, and he knew if he didn't get out soon, hypothermia would set in. What kind of fucking cyborg gets hypothermia?

Just as quickly, he answered his own question. One that was built by a psychopath.

Valenna took off running, and he stiffly followed her as she ran along the length of the tank until she reached its ladder. She gently touched the ladder's grip with a fingertip expecting to get shocked.

She was willing to risk being shocked to pull him out of the water. In that moment, Anders's crush blossomed just a little more.

When she didn't get hurt, she held on to the grips with both hands and hauled herself up the ladder, boots clanging against the metal. She didn't have a flashlight, and she'd never been on the deck before. The very last thing he wanted right now was for her to fall into the tank.

"It's okay," he said, his voice a little steadier. "There's a ladder in here I can use."

"What?"

Damn it. "Don't move," he said. The deck wasn't exactly large; he wasn't sure there was enough space for both of them. "I don't want you to fall in."

"What? I can't hear you." He heard her as she paced the deck's short length, felt the vibrations through the structure and in the water.

Good God. Anders moved closer to the ladder, hands reaching for it, when something crashed into the water.

Not some*thing*. He didn't have to hear Valenna's scream before he moved in her direction, trying to swim with his magnetized boots.

"Fuck!" she shrieked. "It's so *cold*!"

He desperately hoped she knew how to swim. "Kick!" he yelled through the water, but he didn't know if she could hear him over her panicked splashing. "Hold your breath to float!"

He finally got his body to cooperate and made it to the water's surface, fighting against his boots' pull. Valenna flailed in the water, but she wasn't sinking, and as Anders reached for the rope coiled on the furthest end of the deck, he was grateful for that.

"So cold," she said again.

Anders tossed out one end of the rope. "Grab it," he commanded.

She reached for it, missed, and dog-paddled a little closer to the deck. Anders reached for her and hauled her out of the water, hoping his muscles wouldn't freeze up.

He was still holding her against him when they fell to the deck, cushioning her fall.

And now that he was finally out of the water, some of his cybernetic functions felt like they were returning to normal. His body temperature rose, and he could feel his hands and feet again, and his breathing became easier even with Valenna's weight on top of him.

"Are you okay?" he asked.

Through chattering teeth, she said, "Yeah, I think so."

"You came to fish me out," he said.

She nodded. "Yeah."

It was the kindest thing anyone had done for him in years; she was the first person who cared about him since Cecily died.

She didn't move away from him, even though she had to be freezing and needed to get warm as soon as possible. "Your eyes are still glowing," she said, and his heart squeezed painfully at the reminder he wasn't fully human, that he wasn't like her.

"Does it bother you?" he asked.

He didn't know he was holding his breath when she whispered, "No."

Anders didn't think he'd fully forgotten how to read peoples' faces, and she wore a thoughtful expression, like she was trying to decide something. He wondered if he looked the same: he wanted to kiss her but couldn't guess how that would be received.

But she surprised him when her lips met his, so much warmer than he expected, the sensation nearly overwhelming. He responded eagerly, leaning into her, his body heating. Her teeth lightly scraped against his lower lip, and he groaned, his arms pulling her closer.

She raised her head, and he realized her teeth were still chattering.

"Oh, shit," he said. "We have to warm you up."

"Are you feeling better?" she asked.

"Immensely," he replied. She pushed herself off him, water dripping across the deck. "Please be careful. It's slippery. I think Jacoby planned that deliberately." He said those last words quietly but still worried about the bastard barging into the Oasis in a drunken rage.

It had been a long time since he'd gone on a drinking

binge, and he'd never let the installation get to this point when he did before.

Hand-in-hand, he and Valenna gingerly made their way across the deck to the ladder, then back to the floor. "I don't think the base will have hot water right now," he said. "Let's get you back to your barracks with blankets."

She nodded and didn't let go.

They didn't see any sign of Jacoby or the other soldiers as their boots made wet echoes along the corridor floors, and Anders waited to speak until they were safely in her barracks. A single emergency light glowed a few meters from her chosen bunk, illuminating her as she started stripping off her sodden clothes. He averted his eyes, but she suddenly turned around, wet shirt in hand.

"I forgot to stop and get something for you," she said. "Your clothes."

"I'll be fine."

"You can't stay in wet clothes."

"I wasn't planning to."

Even in the dim light, he thought he could see her blush. "There are extra blankets," she said. "And I think I have more stuff I took from the base's storage closets that'll fit you. I didn't bring a lot of stuff when I came here."

He looked away again. The sounds of waterlogged clothing sounded louder than they really were, and he didn't look up again until he'd wrapped a blanket around himself.

She was already in her bunk. "Want to come in?" she asked.

Always. Their kiss wasn't far from his mind. That simple contact would forever remain a treasured memory. He nodded and slid into bed next to her.

"I'm just warming up," she said.

"Me, too."

"Back there?" she said. "I hope I didn't make things weird."

"Never."

"Get warm," she said to herself. "Then find where the other soldiers are and make sure they're okay."

To his shame, Anders had completely forgotten the other grunts while he was in the tank. He saw them so rarely it was easy for their very existence to slip from his mind. "We'll get warm, and then we'll find them," he said. "This isn't the first time Jacoby's gone on a bender. If this binge is like the rest, he'll be out of commission for at least six or eight more hours."

"Okay," she said and snuggled into him a little more. The motion set off a long-forgotten physical reaction, and he pulled away a little.

"What is it?" Valenna asked.

He may as well be honest. "I'm in an awkward position," he said.

Her eyes grew round, and he knew she understood. "Oh."

"Yeah, this is probably the worst time for that to happen."

"Is it me?"

"Are you serious?"

"We were stuck in a freezing cold tank, and we're still trapped on a planet with a psycho and a bunch of mute cyborgs!"

"I like you a lot. We kissed in the Oasis. I'd like to kiss you again. Properly, next time." He paused, unsure if he should be honest. "And yes," he said. "It's you."

"Really?" She sounded astonished, like she couldn't believe she'd be worthy of that.

"Yeah." And as much as his body didn't want to do so, they still had work to do. "But we need to find the other guys first."

CHAPTER 9

"DO you remember where you saw Jacoby?" Anders asked as he dragged a shirt Valenna pilfered from storage over his head. Their clothes were mismatched, but at least they mostly fit. Unfortunately, neither of them had extra boots, so they'd be conducting their espionage in sock feet. Their brief snuggling session in her bunk had to be cut short for the sake of the others.

"It was close to the Oasis," Valenna replied. She tried to remember precisely where. "You know how many doors there are in this place. You don't know where he lives?"

Anders shook his head. "I get to see my room, these barracks, the Oasis, and sometimes the mess if Jacoby's feeling generous. That's it. I haven't even been outside since I got here."

"It's cold and ugly."

"It's cold and ugly in here, too."

"Good point." Valenna stood before the barracks door, trying to decide the best course of action. "Should we split up?"

"I want to say no, but..." He trailed off.

"It'll probably be easier for me to break into places you're not supposed to go," Valenna finished for him. "He can't control me with a switch."

"Yeah." Anders vision was still on night mode, but Valenna forgot about that until he closed his eyes in thought. "I wish you had a weapon."

"It'll be a lot harder to convince Jacoby I don't mean any harm if I have a weapon. And you said he'll be out of commission for the next few hours, anyway."

"I know, I just don't like this."

Both of them stared at the door, and a hundred ways in which all of this could go wrong sailed through Valenna's mind. "Do you know where the other cyborgs are?" she asked.

"I saw where they were on the map," Anders said. "I remember the location. I'll start there first, and I have sensors to help me." He reached for her shoulders, his grip firm and reassuring. "Just try to remember where you saw Jacoby. *Don't* try to be a hero."

"I promise I won't try to be a hero," Valenna said.

Anders didn't look convinced. "I'm serious. He's dangerous and a mean drunk. I don't want him to try to operate on you when he's shitfaced, and I wouldn't put that past him. If you can't find anything, get out, and we'll try another time, okay?"

Valenna hadn't intended to burst into Jacoby's living area with her proverbial guns blazing, but the possibility of being forced into surgery was horrifying, and that was without adding the drunken surgeon. "I promise," she whispered.

"I want to see you back here when I return," Anders said.

"You will."

Anders closed his still-luminescent eyes again, and Valenna already knew what he would do.

This time their kiss was unrushed and sweet, but she still

felt her knees go weak. He held on to her waist to steady her, and in those few seconds she forgot about what they were trying to do, what they needed to do.

She pulled away, wracked with lust and guilt for forgetting about the other soldiers, if only for a few moments.

"Bundle up," Anders said. His voice was a little strangled, and she guessed their kiss had the same effect on him.

"I will." She was already feeling the chill again, and she wished she had a hat to cover her damp hair, now scraped back into a ponytail. She found the jacket she wore when she arrived on Oh-Three-Oh and piled it on over her base-issued sweater. At least it had pockets to keep her hands warm. "Too bad I don't have a flashlight."

"It would draw attention," Anders said. "Just stay in the areas that are as well-lit as possible. And remember what I said."

"Don't be a hero. Right."

"We'll find the other guys, see what we can do to help them, and all work together," Anders said. "It'll be eight against one. We can do this."

They pulled the door apart and stepped into the corridor.

Anders hated to leave Valenna alone, but she swore she wouldn't try anything stupid. He wished he could believe her. After all, she'd tried to pull him out of the water tank.

He hoped that she remembered where she ran into the drunken Jacoby; this place was labyrinthine even to someone like him, whose memory and sense of direction far exceeded unenhanced people.

He'd never used his cybernetics in this kind of situation, and now that he was finally out of the water, he could actually appreciate them. His sensors were on high alert for the first time; it was a much more intense sensation than when he was slowly pacing the tank's floor. Every other sense was piqued as his military training from his pre-cyborg days kicked in. He could be a dangerous son of a bitch if he wanted to be. So could the other guys, if he and Valenna could figure out a way to reprogram them.

He internally cringed at the idea of reprogramming people. That was exactly what Jacoby had done, and that wasn't what cyborgs should be. They'd expected to still be human, only a little faster, a little sharper. Just as Anders felt now.

His vision's data readout alerted him to humanoid life forms in the same area he saw on the screen in Jacoby's lab, startling him. What good did cybernetics serve when cyborgs themselves didn't control them?

Lukas Best ran away to escape the grips of the Zone and its military.

The men he was trying to save couldn't speak.

Anders had spent the last few years pacing a tank, breathing underwater, and for what purpose? So a few planets had an excess of potable water? How, in the name of God, was having amphibian enhancements useful? He was a goddamned *mermaid*.

Valenna might find that funny. In another lifetime, he might, too.

He faced a door, his sensors telling him this was the place. Like everything else on the base, its automatic function was shut off, but at least that meant it would be easier to bypass any biometric locks. He quickly examined the door and locks, looking for the easiest way to break in, and found an emergency latch above the doorway. When he pulled it, the door gave a loud groan that echoed down the corridor, but it opened.

More emergency lights worked in this room, which he

could now see was a barracks like Valenna's. But that was where the similarities ended.

Most of the bunks had been torn out to make way for a long row of adult-sized pods. They reminded Anders of the escape pods used on military craft, and when he peered a little closer at him, he saw they *were* those pods.

What the hell...?

He knew what he would find when he looked through one of the face plates. A man, around his age, if not younger, wide awake and pounding at the plate's plastiglas. Any trace of stoicism the military expected from its grunts was gone, replaced by panic.

"Oh, shit," said Anders. He ran his hands over the pod, looking for the emergency release he knew had to be there. He found it, at its foot, and pushed up the pod's lid.

The soldier bolted from it faster than Anders expected and immediately reached for the release on the pod next to him. Anders followed suit until all six pods were open and their soldiers freed. And not one of them spoke.

Instead, Anders watched as they signed to one another, gestures only they understood. "Hey," he said. He hoped their hearing hadn't been impacted by whatever hideous experiments Jacoby conducted on them.

All six faces turned to look at him. "I'm Captain Anders Barris," he said. It felt weird to be introducing himself using his rank, but hopefully, it would endear himself to them. "I'm a cyborg, too. I've spent the last four years in the water tank in the Oasis." Realizing they had no reason to go in there, and therefore probably didn't know its nickname, he added, "It's what we call that room. Stupid, I know."

His only response was silence.

"The exterior fuel line is broken," Anders said. "And Jacoby's falling-down drunk. We only have a few hours before he sobers up and starts fixing things." He pinned each of them with a stare. "We have to help each other out and find a way off this rock, and we have to do it in a way that Jacoby won't notice."

A few of them exchanged glances, occasionally signing. Finally, one of them tried to clear his throat, then coughed.

The soldier looked up at his fellow grunts, then at Anders. "I think..." he said, voice creaky. He cleared his throat again.

Anders could scarcely believe what he was seeing.

The soldier tried to speak again, this time with more success. His voice, barely a whisper and raspy from disuse, he said, "That's what we've been planning to do."

Valenna stole through the base's darkened corridors, heart pounding so loudly she thought it would rouse Jacoby from wherever he'd conked out. But she saw no one as she rushed through, her footsteps nearly silent.

She'd run into Jacoby near the Oasis, she recalled. In one of the corridors she used all the time. Where the hell was the door he came out of?

She backtracked to the route she'd taken to the Oasis, passing her abandoned cleaning cart along the way. A cleansing cube, its light on standby, ambled its way through the corridor, and when it sensed Valenna, lazily followed her. She ignored it and kept walking.

She stopped under an emergency light that still glowed bright orange, one of the few that did. She was sure she'd seen Dr. Jacoby here.

But there wasn't a door to be found.

Was she losing her mind.

He'd stumbled out of a doorway, she recalled. But it was too dark to see the door clearly. *Did I even see the door?*

Inspiration struck her, and she ran her hands over the

grey-painted walls, looking for a crack or something that would indicate a door.

Hidden in plain sight. It was perfect for someone like Jacoby, all the better to keep his cyborgs from finding him when they finally revolted, and they *would* revolt. Valenna didn't need to be a cyborg to sense the tension surrounding the base.

Her fingers touched a seam in the wall. Despite everything that was happening, excitement thrummed through her at the discovery. She ran her hand along it, up to where a regular door would end, and on her tip-toes, the top of the door.

She'd found it. She just had to remember where it was, exactly.

She patted her pockets, looking for something to mark the spot and came up empty. *God damn it.*

Unless...

She looked up at the emergency light set in the ceiling.

The cleansing cube drifted to her and waited for her to move out of the way so it could disinfect the secret door. Valenna grabbed it and set its functions to manual and pressed its "Idle" button. It beeped, which made her cringe, but stayed in place.

She climbed on top of it and rose to her full height, precariously balanced, her feet taking up most of the space. It dipped but its antigrav functions held, and she shifted a foot a few centimeters over, to press the manual "Lift" button with her toe.

Please let this work.

The cube didn't shoot up to the ceiling as she'd feared but ascended a little more slowly. It beeped again, which Valenna was sure translated to, "Get the hell off me." But it raised her within grabbing distance of the emergency light, which was all she needed.

She wrapped her hands around the emergency light and

pulled with all her might. It popped out of its socket with an ominous hiss and spark, and she hoped she wasn't about to start a fire or set off a klaxon.

To her relief, the socket stayed dark and silent. The cleansing cube beeped again and began to sink. Valenna wasn't a large person, but she supposed cleansing cubes weren't designed to hold adults. At least it wasn't broken.

She hopped off the cube when it was safe to do so and sent it back toward her cleaning cart. She stuffed the hand-sized light in the back waistband of her pants, the only place it would fit, and looked up.

She prayed Jacoby would never notice the missing light.

It wasn't the best marker, but it would have to do.

<hr />

Formosa. Alexander. Johnston. Danvers. Bell. Ralston.

One by one, each of the soldiers introduced himself to Anders, their voices strong and steady through their broadcast link they'd shared with him. A link they'd managed to keep secret from Jacoby, but none of them were sure how long it would be before it was discovered.

"We're not sure how long we have before Jacoby realizes he accidentally reactivated our voice functions," Danvers said through the link. *"We're not used to using them anymore, anyway."*

"How long have you been here?" Anders asked.

"I've been here the longest. Just under four years, I think. The timeline's a little fuzzy."

"Can any of you access the galactic net?"

All of them looked back at him like he was nuts. *"Of course not,"* Formosa replied. *"Do you think we'd be here if we could call for help?"*

"You're being a prick," said Bell. *"He's trying to help us. And*

he's spent the better part of four years in the bottom of a water tank." To Anders, he said, *"How in God's name did you survive the boredom?"*

"I had a good reason to come here," said Anders. *"She's dead now, but there's someone else here who needs to get away before she's turned into a cyborg or forced into motherhood against her will. Everything that's happened to us is inexcusable, but we still signed up for it."*

"Under fraudulent pretences!" snapped Formosa.

"It's different for Valenna," Anders said, surprised how angry his thoughts were, how angry they sounded. *"She was lured here. She was supposed to be here for a few months as a housekeeper and return to her life on Echo-7."* Or wherever she chose to rebuild her life. The point was, she shouldn't be here long term, or subjected to medical experiments.

Formosa stared daggers at him, but he was the only one to do so.

"Valenna's looking for Jacoby's living quarters now," Anders continued. *"We know he definitely has access to the galactic net from somewhere on the base. We have to work together to take him down, bypass any security he put in place on net access, and call for help without alerting the military. It may be easier to get over the border into the Brava System. The war's been over for months."*

No one looked surprised to find out the war was over. Anders doubted any of them cared about it anymore.

"Got it?" Anders asked.

Everyone nodded, including Formosa. But Anders could still feel the man's ire.

He didn't blame him. Anders understood how this looked: that the cyborg in the water tank didn't give a shit about his fellow prisoners until a woman showed up. But that wasn't entirely the case, and as he ran through plans of attack and escape through his mind, he hoped they would see things as he did.

CHAPTER 10

THE POWER still hadn't been restored by the time Valenna slunk back to her barracks. She crawled into bed, fully dressed to ward off the cold, and waited for Anders. Would he come back? What if they'd been wrong about the other cyborgs; what if they'd been programmed to react violently to any suggestion that went against Dr. Jacoby's orders?

Lukas Best had circumvented any violent tendencies inserted into his programming, but he'd been a prototype as far as Valenna knew, the only official cyborg success story. Prototypes were bound to have some bugs.

She cringed inwardly at her thoughts, particularly those toward Lukas. She didn't blame him for despising her.

He and Cressida were so *happy* together.

She didn't resent them for it—God and the stars knew they both deserved a little happiness—but their relationship was a stark reminder of everything Valenna wrecked in her life.

She had an opportunity now to help save some of the other victims of the military's cyborg program, if that's what they were. The more she thought about it, the more she was sure Jacoby's experiments weren't officially sanctioned by the Zone or its military.

It's corrupt as all hell, but is it that *corrupt?*

She couldn't think of an answer to that question.

Her chronometer told her it was nearly nine in the evening, but she didn't feel tired at all. She still wrapped herself in scratchy military-issue blankets, trying to convince herself that everything would be okay.

She was wide awake when the barracks door scraped open. Heart in her throat, she waited to see who would stick his head in the doorway. Relief poured through her when she saw who it was.

Anders slipped in and hauled the door shut behind him, then squeezed into Valenna's narrow bunk beside her. "How did it go?" she asked.

He tapped his head. "We're all on the same wavelength now, and I think I mean that literally."

He quickly told her about finding the other cyborgs locked in modified military escape pods, how he'd helped them out and then back in after their meeting to throw off any suspicions Jacoby might have about them. They'd figured out a way to communicate with one another, in an almost telepathic way, and linked in Anders.

His story was incredible. He'd made amazing progress with reaching out to the other cyborgs and making them allies. So she felt a little foolish explaining her small victory in their recon mission, shyly producing the pilfered emergency light from its hiding spot under one of the unused bunks' pillows.

But Anders looked at her like she was a genius. "You know where he's hiding," he said.

"Well, not really," she protested. "I found it again by chance. And I'm really hoping he doesn't remember that he stumbled out of there today or it'll mess up everything we have planned." She paused. "What *do* we have planned, exactly?"

"We get access to the galactic net," Anders said. "Then we get a message out for help. There are a few options for that, all civilian, according to the guys. It's just a matter of who can get to Oh-Three-Oh the fastest and without the military being alerted."

"What about Dr. Jacoby? It's not like he'll let his experiments just sail away."

Valenna already knew the answer to her question, was dreading it, but she was still surprised when Anders replied.

"We're still going to kill him."

Neither of them spoke much after Anders's pronouncement. Valenna didn't know what to say. It wasn't like she could talk him out of killing Jacoby, and when she thought about it a little more, she wasn't sure she wanted to. The man was a monster.

But wasn't *she* a monster, too, albeit of a different type?

Hell, she was here to make herself less of a monster.

She leaned against Anders, both of them swaddled in blankets against the cold, unsure what to talk about next. "Has the power ever gone out before?" she asked.

"Not like this." He hesitated, as if what he wanted to say next might upset her.

"What is it?"

"For a little while, it crossed my mind that this might be a test."

Valenna felt herself go numb in a way that had nothing to do with the chill. "What?"

"Jacoby seeing what we would do if we had free rein of the installation," he said. "I wouldn't put it past him."

"Do you think that now?"

"The power's been out for hours," Anders replied. "It's getting colder. Jacoby doesn't have the ability to regulate his temperature the way we do."

"Neither do I."

"Yeah, but you have me." In the light emitted from his eyes, she thought she could see a smile on his face. Just as quickly, it was gone. "Does it bother you we're probably going to have to kill him?"

"A little," she admitted. "I get it, but it's still hard to think about."

He paused again. "Didn't you ever see anyone die when...?" His voice trailed off.

Valenna's heart squeezed painfully in her chest. "A few times," she said. "But that was darfin overdose, not..." She nearly said, "murder," but she didn't think killing Jacoby should fit the word's definition. "Self-defense," maybe. "When it happened, it was early on when I started using. We were all pretty ignorant at first about potency," she continued.

Anders was quiet for a moment, probably digesting what she'd told him. It felt weird to talk about her early darfin days: the tantalizing, sugary smell of the sticky patches she'd affix to her arms, the rush that left her delightfully dizzy without a care in the world, lurching around a friend's dismal apartment that turned into a wonderland once the high set in.

Then later on, when its allure wore off, and she became dependent on it. She constantly scratched the bleeding rashes that covered her body from darfin patches, her heart raced so quickly she thought she might have a coronary from withdrawal. She still recalled the shame she felt when she slept with one of her dealers in exchange for more patches when she was short on scrip. She'd robbed Cressida for stuff to pawn when she didn't want to sell her body for it, even though Cressida's lifestyle was hardly extravagant.

"Do you want to talk about it?" Anders finally asked.

"It sucked," Valenna said shortly. "I did a lot of things I regret."

"Everyone has," Anders said gently.

"You're a soldier," she replied. "And you didn't just enlist, you *volunteered* to be a cyborg guinea pig for your sister. I robbed mine and then set a bounty hunter after her. You still tried to save her, and I know you beat yourself up a lot because she didn't make it, but you still did your best. More than your best. And now you're trying to get everyone off this rock back to safety. You're a hero, you know that?"

He was quiet again, and Valenna wondered if she'd offended him when she reiterated that Cecily had died. Or maybe he finally realized that she really was the horrible person she knew herself to be and would focus his rescue efforts on the other cyborgs, who deserved redemption.

"I think," Anders said slowly, "That you're having trouble reconciling the person you used to be with the person you are now. You've changed for the better."

Valenna was motionless, hardly daring to breathe, waiting for him to continue.

"You came here to pay off old debts and keep your sister safe," Anders said. "You're actively helping all of us escape now that we know what's going on. You could just sit on your ass and wait for rescue, but you aren't. You took big risks getting one of the other guys to open up to you and then marking Jacoby's hidden door. You didn't have to do that."

His kind words brought tears to her eyes. "But I did," she whispered.

"You didn't," he insisted. "You chose to. You made some terrible decisions before, but you're trying to be a better person now, and you're succeeding."

Valenna wiped away an errant tear. "Thank you."

He tipped a finger under her chin, bringing her face closer to his, all the better to look her in the eye. The glow in his eyes was reassuring, almost like a nightlight. She bit back a smile at the comparison.

"What is it?" he asked.

"Your eyes," she said, then quickly added, "They're comforting, you know? You're telling me I'm this strong, good person, but I feel protected."

"You're not bothered by the cyborg thing?"

"Of course not." An ugly memory popped into her mind, unbidden: taking off from Haven, Cressida and Lukas cuffed to worn-out seats aboard Janek Dalton's death trap of a ship. Valenna could still remember the horrible things she'd said to them, word for word, and how she'd stumbled out of the cabin where they were confined to slap half of a darfin patch on her lower back to take the edge off her withdrawal.

She hadn't been truly bothered by Lukas being a cyborg. She'd been bothered and jealous when she saw just how fucking *happy* Cressida was with him. Her sister was angry and devastated at being hauled away from Haven, but even someone like Valenna had seen the love between them. So Valenna had said the most hurtful things she could think of.

Cressida had something else to live for besides keeping up with her rent and air bills. So had Valenna, but it was more expensive than either of those things and would have killed her if she hadn't quit. Or the dealers would have killed her.

"I don't care you're a cyborg," she reiterated. "That doesn't change the fact that you're one of the nicest people I've ever met. You could just overpower Jacoby and find a way off here and damn the rest of us. You have the strength to do that."

"About that," Anders said. "I was in the Oasis today because I mouthed off to Jacoby about—well, about everything. That's probably why he got drunk. And I'll be going back in the tank when he sobers up, and I don't know for how long this time. I've never done that before."

Valenna read between the lines: he would be punished, and it would be worse than ever.

"He can control me remotely," Anders said. "That's how

he forced me into the tank today, otherwise I would've just cut all our losses and taken care of him in the lab."

She didn't know when she would get to spend time with him again if Jacoby was in the mood Anders said he was in. Without him, finding a way off Oh-Three-Oh would fall on her and the other cyborgs.

"You'll be in there a while," she said. "And he'll probably keep you cold."

"I'll be fine," he said. "I always am, I promise. He still needs me for research purposes."

For research purposes. Valenna hated the way those words sounded.

He was willing to subject himself to days in the tank, for the sake of everyone else on this godforsaken planet. For the other cyborgs. For her.

He knew who and what she was and still cared about her. Valenna didn't remember the last time that had happened.

She closed the small distance between them, her kiss urgent. He immediately responded, pulling her against him, tongue teasing her lips apart. Desire reared its head in her, demanding and impatient, and for a few glorious seconds as his hands pushed aside layers of her clothes to rest against the bare skin of her back, she forgot all about what was still in store for them.

He was so *warm*. His touch still had her breath stuttering against his lips, the sensation nearly overwhelming. She hadn't been touched with any kind of affection for longer than she cared to admit, and it had been even longer since she wanted to touch someone else.

He paused. "You don't have to do anything you don't want to," he murmured against her lips.

"But I do," she whispered. "I want you. I would even if we weren't here."

Every word of that was true. Her mind flashed back to the

first time she saw him in the Oasis: this strong man, unafraid of anything, standing in the water, the tank's safety lights illuminating him like some kind of brawny angel.

And then he'd turned out to be a kind man who cared about other people, including her. She'd never be worthy of that affection, but she'd always crave it.

His fingers traced circles on her back in a gesture that was both exciting and reassuring. Valenna pulled away from him enough to pull her myriad sweaters and tank top over her head. Anders's luminescent eyes, now half-hooded, took in the sight with a look that already had her toes curling.

"You're sure about this?" he breathed.

She nodded. "Very sure."

"You'll get cold."

She shrugged and reached for the clasp on her bra and shrugged it off. "I'm sure you'll keep me warm."

That was all the encouragement Anders needed. He let go of her enough to strip off his own shirt, then pulled her against him, urging her to straddle his body. Valenna gasped at the heat their skin shared, so much better than that offered by scratchy blankets.

There was a sense of urgency shared between them, as if they didn't know how long they had before Anders was summoned. And they didn't know how long they had, Valenna thought, as his fingers worked the seal on her oversized trousers. But the sadness at that knowledge evaporated when, her pants apparently forgotten, he took the tip of her breast in his mouth. She couldn't keep a small cry from escaping her, and his responding groan spurred her own desire.

Even before her darfin days, she'd never experienced roiling lust like this.

But the part of her brain that was still rational chided her a little. *It's not just lust. You really care about this man.*

He cared about her, too. And that was thrilling and exciting rather than scary.

Anders's mouth found hers again, and those rational thoughts finally dissipated like a wisp of smoke. This time it was her turn to pluck at Anders's remaining clothes with an immediacy she'd never felt before. She needed to be as close to him as possible, keep him near her for as long as she could.

He seemed to understand her urgency, and in a few seconds, both of them were freed from their clothes, and Valenna tugged the blankets a little higher around her shoulders.

"Cold?" he asked.

"I'm trying not to be."

In one swift motion, he flipped her on her back. He braced her hands on either side of her head and laced his fingers through hers. "Better?"

She was surrounded by him, his cyborg body heat warming her in a way the blankets couldn't. "Yes."

His knee urged her legs apart, erection bobbing against her thigh, his mouth finding the sensitive spot on her neck and lightly biting it. A shiver of anticipation raced through her at the thought of what would happen next.

He settled against the cradle of her hips, a teasing gesture that she would have protested had every one of her body's senses not overpowered her ability to speak. When he finally thrust into her, all she could do was let out a mewl of relief, silenced by a hard kiss.

Her hips lifted to meet his, urging him on, stoking the fire that was already building in her veins. When her climax crashed over her, she didn't have the presence of mind to muffle her cry, and the sound seemed to hasten his.

They lay entwined in the darkness, breaths still coming fast. Wordlessly, Anders rolled on his side, taking her with him, and pressed a kiss to her forehead, a surprisingly sweet gesture.

As they drifted off to sleep, bathed in the emergency lights' dim glow, all Valenna could think about was what was ahead for them, how she would never stop fighting for Anders.

CHAPTER 11

ANDERS WAS awake before Valenna stirred. The emergency lights were still on, and the barracks room still cold, telling him that the installation's power wasn't yet restored. He ran a quick diagnostic on himself and found that everything was working as it should.

He could find the spot with the missing emergency light, break through the wall, and kill Jacoby. Hell, the other guys would be happy to help; if nothing else, they'd push him aside for the chance to tear him limb from limb.

He cast a quick glance at Valenna, who looked more peaceful than she ever had and jettisoned the idea. If it was just him, he'd kill Jacoby and figure everything else out later, but it wasn't just him. He'd promised the others he wouldn't make a move without them. They needed to be working in tandem for a successful escape to happen.

Guilt wracked through him at the thought of the others, sealed in their modified pods while he made love to Valenna. But she'd been right last night when she said neither of them knew how long they had until Jacoby did whatever sadistic thing to him next. Anders would not regret the time he'd spent with her.

He brushed a lock of dark hair away from her face. "Hey," he said softly.

She stirred, dark eyes blinking. "Good morning," she said. She craned her head to look around the room. "I guess everything's still shut down."

"I need to get back to the Oasis," he said.

She sat up in bed, blankets held against her bare skin. He still saw goosebumps form in the room's chill. "Are you sure?" she whispered. "We could make a move today." She paused. "What time is it?"

"Oh-five-hundred hours," Anders replied. "And I think we need to act like everything is normal until we can get reliable access to Jacoby's quarters. That'll be a team effort. All of us need to be on board with that. I can't do it alone." When she opened her mouth to protest, he added, "Not you. You're going to stay out of the crossfire, and if a chance comes up for you to escape before we take care of Jacoby, you need to take it."

"That's unlikely."

"But if it happens, do it," he said. He took her face in his hands, brushing the pads of his thumbs over her cheekbones. "Promise me."

She rolled her eyes but said, "I promise I'll abandon you and the other cyborgs if the opportunity to save my own ass at your expense comes up."

"I'm going to ignore the sarcasm, but thank you." He kissed her, putting as much of his emotion for her in it as he could.

He got out of bed. "I'll get something solid to eat," he said. "Then I'm going back to the Oasis. I don't think it's a good idea if we're together for that. God only knows what Jacoby's going to do or say when his hangover wears off. Wait half an hour, and then get your breakfast and start working again.

"I don't like it when you tell me what to do," she grumbled, but she lay back against the pillows.

"I'm sure you don't, but I *was* a captain, once upon a time," Anders pointed out. "I used to give orders."

She turned on her side to face him, levering herself up one elbow. "I'm not military."

"I know you aren't. The military was never that hot."

That earned a smile from her, at least. But it quickly faded. "Please be careful. I don't know what else to say to you, but I need you alive and in one piece, okay?"

"I promise I won't let Jacoby pick me apart and sell me to a scrapyard."

She sat up again, horror across her face. "Oh, my God! That wasn't what I meant!"

"I know it wasn't. I was trying to tease you and I failed at it."

She relaxed a little. "Look, just stay alive. Remember that you aren't the only person who'll help you fight back."

He finished pulling his clothes on and walked back to the bed, sitting down next to her. He took in every detail of her face: her wide eyes and the shadows beneath them, the angle of her cheekbones, the full lips he would never tire of kissing. He wasn't sure when he would get this close to her again.

"I'll remember," he said. And with that, he kissed her goodbye and left the barracks.

———

Valenna waited until a half hour had passed according to her chronometer before getting out of bed.

She quickly dressed, gathered her things, and wrenched open the barracks door, looking up and down the still-darkened corridors, but there wasn't a sign of life. She stole down the corridor in sock feet for the shower room, knowing it was probably going to be cold, but she needed it to wake up and get her bearings.

A single emergency light glowed in the empty shower room, and she picked the first stall and turned on the water. Bracing herself, she stood under its spray, pleasantly surprised when it turned out to be only a little chillier than lukewarm. She was still quick, and in a few minutes had dressed in fresh clothes.

What to do next?

She wandered to the mess, but there wasn't power for the replicators to run. She found a stash of protein cubes and ate one, then went off in search of her cleaning cart. She may as well get some work done before Jacoby made his next grand entrance.

As she paced through the corridors, another thought struck her. What if he drank himself to death? He'd been stumbling last night, definitely drunk. But not lethally so, as far as she could tell, but Valenna had never been much of a drinker. Didn't people in the deepest throes of alcohol poisoning usually pass out? Anders had said his binges had happened before.

But it only takes one fatal overdose, right?

Valenna activated the cleaning cart—at least that still worked—and it trailed behind her as she stalked the installation's corridors, looking for the cleansing cube she used to boost herself the night before.

She'd left the light in one of the beds. She doubted Jacoby would think to look for it there if he notices it was gone.

She quickly glanced at the ceiling, two-and-a-half meters above her head, at the rows of emergency lights, many of them flickering or burned out. It was very possible Jacoby would never notice one was missing.

She found the cleansing cube close to where she'd removed the light, near Jacoby's hideaway. When she squinted at the wall, she could see the faint lines where a doorway was indicated, one that couldn't be easily accessed from the corridor. Where the hell did he get into his apartment?

She'd have to find out later. Right now, she had to get the cube away from the door.

It drifted back to the cleaning cart, and she affixed it to the side along with a cluster of other cleansing cubes. She quickly turned around and left that part of the corridor, on the chance Jacoby came across her.

She walked until she felt she was a safe distance away, then checked the thincomp Jacoby issued her on her first day. According to it, she was supposed to clean the mess first thing, so she went back and set the cleansing cubes to disinfect the tabletops. She mopped the floor and wished for a hot cup of tea.

Not just that. She wished she and Anders could find their way off Oh-Three-Oh, for the chance to punch Janek Dalton in the face for bringing her here, for a better relationship with Cressida and Lukas.

She swallowed a watery sigh and plunked down at one table, watching a cube aim its lasers on the replicator's darkened menu screen.

Poor Anders.

If not for her, he and the others could've tracked down and killed Jacoby already.

He's doing all of this for me.

Despite her fear over what the next days would bring, a warm, fuzzy feeling flowed through her when she thought of Anders. He knew what she was, what she'd done, and he still cared about her. She hadn't intended for the events of the night before to happen, but they had, and she was glad for that. She would treasure that memory forever. She felt a smile ghost her lips.

It quickly evaporated when she heard footsteps in the corridor. She quickly stood up and waited.

Just as she suspected, it was Jacoby. Loathing washed through her at the sight, and she schooled her face into a neutral expression. "Hi," she said cautiously. "Are you feeling better this morning?"

He certainly didn't look it. His hair stuck up at odd angles and he still wore the same clothes from the night before, minus his lab coat. His cheeks were sunken and eyes shadowed by half-moons. He looked like hell.

"It'll pass," he said gruffly. He looked around the mess. "You're working?"

She nodded. "I didn't know what else to do." She held her breath, waiting for his next words.

But his shoulders slumped. "Of course, you are," he said. "It's nice that *someone* around here pays attention." He gave her a fake smile that showed too much teeth, and Valenna suppressed a shiver. "The power will be restored today."

She nodded. "Glad to hear that. It's a little cold today."

"This whole fucking rock is cold, isn't it?"

The profanity took Valenna aback, but she didn't comment on it.

Jacoby continued to surprise her when he lumbered into the mess and sat down heavily at the table. "I apologize for last night," he said. "I don't usually behave in such a way."

"We all have bad days," Valenna said, then added, "I guess it's worse for someone who doesn't have a colleague to lean on."

She hoped she hadn't overstepped her bounds.

"That's just it," Jacoby said. "I have reason to believe the colleague I relied on is no longer among the living."

"I'm sorry to hear that, sir."

"Me, too." Was it her imagination, or did he look a little

desolate? "I don't have confirmation yet. I would have to leave and do my own investigation for that to get it."

Valenna knew she was treading on dangerous territory and parsed her words carefully. "Is there anyone who can check up on your friend?"

"No. I don't even know the precise location of his research lab," Jacoby lamented. "He felt it was safer that way."

"Safer, sir?"

His bloodshot eyes pinned her with a hard stare. "Did you *really* think what we're doing is sanctioned by the government?"

She felt sick. She'd known what was happening here wasn't legal, but he'd just confirmed it. Still, she continued to play dumb. "Dr. Jacoby, I was high most of the time until just over a year ago. I left school when I was fifteen." She forced out a small, humorless laugh. "I'm not exactly in the know when it comes to the government."

"I suppose not," Jacoby said. "I've been trying to get in touch with Colton for days. *Weeks*. I've pinged every transmit address I have for him and nothing's happened. I got in touch with some of his other colleagues and they informed me he went AWOL months ago." He turned beseeching eyes to Valenna. "He's dead."

"Colton?"

"Colton Byers. His name, you idiot." Jacoby tried to stand up, but his legs wouldn't support him. He wobbled back into his seat. "We worked in research and development together on the military's official cyborg project at Caron Cybernetics. When it was discontinued, we decided to conduct our own research privately."

Valenna waited for him to continue, not wanting to interrupt and remind him of who he was really speaking to.

"He made incredible progress on nanobot technology,"

Jacoby said. "Absolutely remarkable. And he successfully created a nanobot-reliant cyborg."

Before she could stop herself, Valenna prompted, "And you haven't?"

"I'm working on it. I need a younger test subject. Byers had an older child, but, well..." He closed his eyes. "The child's probably dead now if Byers is."

"Oh, my God," Valenna whispered. She felt sick.

That poor kid. Everything kept getting worse and worse.

Jacoby slammed his hands on the tabletop, making her jump. "I have to get back to work," he said, again to himself. "Get this shitpile back up and running. Keep doing what you're doing, Valenna."

He left the room without so much as a goodbye, not that Valenna would have been able to muster one.

She couldn't believe what she'd just learned, what she would be able to tell Anders the next time she saw him.

But she also understood again, with horrifying clarity, that knowing what she did meant that Jacoby would never let her leave Oh-Three-Oh alive.

———

Valenna dragged the cleaning cart around the installation, pretending to work. Occasionally she would set a cube loose in a random area, but that was all she could do. She discovered the water had stopped running when she tried to refill her mop bucket, which gave her something else to worry about.

And was it getting even *colder*? Was Oh-Three-Oh entering its winter season?

She didn't see Jacoby, Anders, or the other cyborgs during her wandering, and after a few hours, the loneliness finally got to her. She directed the cart to the Oasis, determined to get a glimpse of Anders, if only for her own selfish reasons.

She could barely make out his shape in the tank, sitting down and with his back to her. She thought about tapping on the plastiglas, making her presence known, but something stopped her. She'd never seen him hunched over in such a way, like all of his will to live had been sapped away by the water.

But the sliver of light spilling into the Oasis from the lab offered a distraction. She paused, unsure of what to do next.

"Dr. Jacoby?" she called.

That got Anders's attention. He turned around, his vision on full glow. He made a shooing motion with his hands.

Valenna ignored him and crept toward the lab. "Dr. Jacoby?"

The emergency lights in here were brighter, casting the equipment inside in terrifying relief. But Jacoby was nowhere in sight.

A thincomp was tossed on the diagnostic bed. A familiar thincomp, its screen a web of cracks. Valenna hadn't seen it since it was confiscated her first night here.

Was this a trick? She glanced around the room, then stuck her head in the Oasis, ears straining for Jacoby's footsteps, but she heard nothing other than her own rapid breathing.

She might never get such a chance again. She grabbed her thincomp and nearly cried when it activated at her touch.

The galactic net! I can get to it!

This time a few tears escaped her. With shaking fingers, she opened her messages, heart leaping in her throat when she saw most of them were from Cressida. She didn't have time to read or watch them, so she pulled up her sister's transmit address and typed in a quick note.

I'm trapped on Omega-Three-Omega with seven cyborgs. Janek Dalton brought me here. Dr. Jacoby turned them. Send help. I love you, Cressy. I'm sorry.

She didn't let herself breathe until she saw the message was successfully sent, and she hoped that was enough information for Cressida to go on. She erased all traces of it from the device and checked the rest of the outbound messages. It appeared Jacoby had tried repeatedly tried to get in touch with Colton Byers, and the top outbounder raged at the man for not responding, and how dare he not do so when his project was falling apart, his equipment was rotting, even his thincomps were shorting out from age. That explained why he'd used hers.

Valenna replaced the thincomp exactly where she found it, and slipped out of the lab.

She made it out of the Oasis and back into the corridor before she saw Jacoby again. He looked just as haggard as he had earlier, and even more pissed off. "Everything all right?" she stammered.

"Of course not," he snapped.

"I know, but how are repairs going?" Her words came out in a rush, and she inwardly cursed herself for it. She was acting guilty.

"The grunts are out there, fixing the exterior fuel lines," he said, waving his hand dismissively. "They *are* obedient, I'll give them that."

Because you programmed them to be, you sick fuck. She nodded. "Any guess when the power will be back on?"

He gave a half-hearted shrug. "Maybe an hour, maybe less. I'm sure Barris will appreciate some warm water again." He jerked his thumb in the Oasis's direction.

"Yeah, about that." *Here goes nothing.* "What's the point of leaving him in there?"

"Warfare research. It's also entirely possible that I can enhance a soldier to where they could perform their duties in open space."

She couldn't keep her jaw from dropping at that pronouncement. Even Valenna knew that was far outside the realm of possibility for humanoids, cyborgs or not.

But she collected herself before replying. "I can see how that would be useful."

"It would be easier to make those modifications in an infant," Jacoby said.

God damn it, he was back to the baby thing. Her mind flashed back to the night before, and with it, a corresponding anger at what she and Anders shared being used for such a horrific experiment.

"That's a big decision," she said, trying to keep her voice light. "I'm still thinking about it. And this place isn't equipped for a baby, anyway."

Her mind worked rapidly. She knew almost nothing about children, and she grasped at the tidbits of information she had. "Even a cyborg baby needs somewhere to play," she said. "And fresh air. This place doesn't even have windows. There's also nutrition to think of. For me and any baby I have. I need more than protein cubes if I'm going to grow a whole person."

Jacoby considered all of this for a few seconds. "Of course," he said. "I'd take care of all of that."

"So you see where my concerns are coming from," Valenna said. "I get you're doing important research, but right now, this is the worst possible place to raise a kid." She heard one of the cleansing cubes beeping somewhere down the corridor. "I have to get that," she said, and quickly began walking away. Thank God for finicky cubes. "Don't bother to tell me when the power's back on," she called over her shoulder. "I'll know."

CHAPTER 12

ANDERS DIDN'T MOVE when he heard Valenna leave the Oasis, nor when the vibrations of her voice carried over to him through the plastiglas and water when she spoke to Jacoby. He listened, just in case she needed his help.

But she didn't. He didn't know what she'd done when she dared to venture into the lab, and while he wanted to, he couldn't very well ask about it right now. He could only hope that whatever she had done hadn't endangered herself.

But Jacoby merely dismissed her and stalked back into the Oasis, muttering something about "useless fucking staff" under his breath.

They aren't useless, you sadistic fuck.

One of the cyborgs' voices popped into his mind; he recognized it as belonging to Formosa. *"Everything okay in there, old man?"*

Damn it. Anders hadn't meant to broadcast that thought. He was used to shielding them from Jacoby, but having his mind connected to the other cyborgs was something else entirely. *"Yeah, everything's about as fine as it can be. How is it out there?"* As an afterthought, he added, *"I'm thirty. I'm not that much older than you."*

The other cyborgs were outside, conducting repairs on the installation's damaged fuel reserve and lines. Apparently, there had been a vicious storm the day before that the structure completely muffled, accounting for the outage.

Formosa had been the one to show him the night before how to access the link he and the others had created to communicate with each other. After that, Anders was hit with a barrage of information: schematics of the base they'd compiled, dossiers on the other cyborgs and Jacoby, even the scant information they had about Lukas Best. And, most importantly, their escape plan, now that Anders told them where Jacoby's hidey-hole was.

"Thirty's older than any of us, so you're old," Formosa said. *"We're temporarily compelled to stay out here until we're done with the repairs. Our plan is the same, though: now that we know where Jacoby sleeps, we can storm his quarters, kill him, access the galactic net, and find a way off here. Your girlfriend told you the war's over. We can hide in the Brava System indefinitely."*

"My girlfriend?" It took Anders a few seconds to remember that he was still connected to the rest of the cyborgs.

"Thanks for tuning out of the link last night when you did, by the way, if only to keep the rest of us from getting jealous."

"Oh, shit." Valenna would *not* be happy to hear about that, even if the link he shared with the other cyborgs was broken when it was. *"Sorry about that."*

"No worries, we didn't hear anything incriminating. Fuck!"

Anders straightened, the water swirling. *"Everything all right?"*

"Just some sparks I wasn't expecting. Look, about Valenna, just don't forget what's important. We've been here for a long time, and we didn't consent to everything that's happened so far."

"Valenna hasn't consented to being an incubator, either."

"Good point. The other point to remember is, don't forget about the rest of us."

"Give me more credit than that, please." But even as he "spoke" the words, he had to think about who he would save if it came down to making a choice. It killed him he couldn't answer who it would be.

"Just reminding you, old man."

The link was quiet for a few moments, then he heard Formosa again. *"Keep quiet about this, Captain,"* the cyborg said. *"We've accidentally connected to the galactic net."*

Anders tried to rise to his feet, but he'd been sitting on the tank's floor so long it was a struggle. Trying to keep his composure and any suspicion off himself, he slowly paced its floor, getting more feeling into his legs and feet. *"Are you shitting me?"*

"Not in the least. Johnston's sending out an SOS now before Jacoby finds out what happened and cuts off the access from wherever he's hiding." Formosa paused. *"You know that not all of us may make it out alive?"*

Anders swallowed the lump that formed in his throat. *"Yeah."*

Valenna needed to live. She hadn't signed up for any of this; she'd just wanted to earn enough money as a housekeeper to start her life over.

"What the hell?"

Anders hadn't known it was possible to sound incredulous as much as Formosa had during their short conversation. *"What's wrong?"*

"Valenna found a connection to the galactic net. She sent out a message."

Ander's spirits soared, pride surging through him. She'd done it! Just as quickly, dread replaced his elation. *"You wouldn't know if Jacoby noticed?"*

"Nothing I can see yet, but I don't think we'll be able to hack into the connections too much without him noticing." There was a pause, then Formosa said, *"I caught and copied the message. I'm sending it to you now."*

Words replaced Anders's vision, a short message Valenna had written to Cressida. She wrote where she was, that there were others who needed rescuing, that she was sorry.

Anders shrugged even though Formosa couldn't see the gesture. *"I see nothing wrong with what she sent. Her sister has a connection that could help us."* Surely Lukas Best would want to help his cyborg brothers, wouldn't he?

"It'll be nice if help arrives, but it probably won't in time for what we're going to do. Any sign of Jacoby?"

Anders slowly rotated around the tank, his night vision activated. He was the only person in the Oasis. *"That's a negative."*

"He'll show up sooner rather than later, I'm sure." There was another pause. *"Power's restored in five ... four ... three ... two ... one."*

The Oasis's lights cycled on, and from elsewhere in the base, engines resumed whirring, the noise after hours of silence almost deafening.

The lights flashed on and a blast of warm air shot out from the ceiling, eliciting a shriek of surprise from Valenna. Heart pounding, she caught her breath, and despite all that was happening, she couldn't help but smile in relief.

The power's back on. Thank God.

It had been a few hours since she sent her plea for help to Cressida, and Jacoby hadn't come looking for her, so she hoped that meant she was in the clear for now. Not that she expected it to last. Either Cressida would show up, or Jacoby found out what she'd done, but for now, she would relax a little and pray that the universe was on her side.

She heard familiar stomping down the corridor, outside the mess where she was finally enjoying a hot cup of tea. She braced herself.

"Everything's restored," Jacoby said as he strode into the room.

"Good thing. I was getting cold."

Jacoby harrumphed a little at that pronouncement. "We're getting a delivery tonight. It's a little early, but it works out since we're short on everything. My thincomps are all out of commission."

Valenna kept her expression neutral. "You could use mine," she offered, pointing to her cleaning cart waiting in the corner.

"It can't connect to ..." Jacoby caught himself before he finished, but Valenna was sure he was about to say, "the galactic net." "It doesn't connect well to the base's internal network," he said instead. "No multitasking. It's an older model."

"Well, yeah. Wouldn't want to risk a late model thincomp getting wet or lasered by a cube, right?" Valenna forced out a laugh.

He looked at her like she was crazy. "Just a joke," Valenna said quietly.

He blinked, then shook his head a little. "Right. Sorry, I haven't heard one in a while."

"Especially a bad one," Valenna said.

Stop babbling, you idiot!

But if Jacoby had noticed her nervousness, he didn't let on. He was too preoccupied with something else, and she desperately prayed that he hadn't figured out what the cyborgs were planning.

Hell, even *she* didn't know what the cyborgs were

planning. Anders had refused to tell her in the morning, only insisting that she escape if she ever got the chance. She *hated* being out of the loop.

But if Jacoby knew that the installation's cyborgs had something planned, he didn't let on. Instead, an unusually thoughtful expression crossed his face. "Have you ever lost someone close to you?"

Was this a conversation opener into threatening Cressida? Valenna sincerely hoped not. "Well, you read all the information available about me," she said carefully. "I'm sure there was something in there about my parents. I never did find out what happened to my dad."

Center City alone was home to millions of people, in a system holding billions of people. It was very easy for someone of her father's social standing or lack of thereof, to disappear and never be found if he didn't want to be. Valenna knew he got sick of looking after his small children and darfin-dependent wife and took off. It was a common enough story when she was growing up.

Jacoby waved his hand dismissively at the mention of her father, and what remained of Valenna's spirits sank. Part of her had hoped her dossier included information on her dad's fate, but evidently not. "Sorry, I wasn't especially close to my parents. Just to the friend of mine I told you about, whom I'm quite certain is dead."

"Byers, right? I'm sorry to hear that." But if he'd been working toward the same monstrous aims as Jacoby, she was glad to hear of the friend's demise.

Jacoby shook his head a little. "Well, Colton's research days are over."

"Maybe he took a vacation," Valenna said.

"Doubtful. There's always research to be done." He pinched the bridge of his nose between his fingers and squeezed his eyes shut. When he opened them, he looked around the mess, then at Valenna, and sighed. "Take the rest of the day off."

"Are you sure?"

"Are you saying you don't want the rest of the day off?"

"No," she said quickly. Thinking about the lab and his hidden apartment, she blurted, "Isn't there anything else I could help you with? Any cleanup from the power outage?"

"That's what the soldiers are taking care of."

"What about Captain Barris?"

Those were the wrong words to say because a flicker of interest crossed Jacoby's face. "You've made your decision about what we discussed?"

That he still thought a baby was possible after Valenna's history of darfin use was almost laughable, but she didn't want him to get the idea to operate on her to fix her reproductive issues or use those nanobots on her again. "Well, it's Captain Barris's decision, too."

"He's a cyborg," Jacoby said. "It isn't as though he has much of a choice in the matter."

Valenna understood his subtext and hated it. But she said, "Well, I'm open to it, but I'd still like Captain Barris to be on board with the idea." She hoped they were out of there before Jacoby became more insistent on her having a baby.

"You'd never make it as a research scientist," Jacoby said, but he spoke the words almost affectionately.

She pointed to the cleaning cart and forced a smile on her face. "Guess it's a good thing I already have a career."

Even though his cybernetic enhancements meant he should be impervious to cold, Captain Jason Formosa still felt the chill. Or thought he could. Maybe it was the human side of him that still insisted on shivering just because he was supposed to.

Or maybe it was Oh-Three-Oh's increased gravity relative to that supported in the installation or any other planet in the Zone he'd been to, knocking him off-kilter somehow. Or it could be the fact that he and the rest of his silenced comrades had been outside the base for over thirteen hours at this point, and it was the middle of the night and colder than ever. Omega-Three-Omega was heading into its brutal, lethally cold winter season.

What did it matter anyway? He was still more machine than man.

"Do you hear that?"

Corporal Johnston's mental voice broke through his self-pity, and he snapped back to attention. At least the feed line he'd been tinkering with was repaired. *"Sorry, what was that?"* All he could hear was the rush of wind in his ears, a sure sign of another storm. The sky was already gray, and a few snowflakes whirled around his head.

"Dude, come on," said Johnston. *"You can't feel the vibrations?"*

Formosa paused and focused on their surroundings and quickly heard and felt what Johnston was talking about. The roar of heavy air engines was growing louder, eclipsing the wind rushing through his ears.

"Was Jacoby expecting a delivery?" Johnston asked.

"How the fuck should I know?" Formosa replied, then immediately felt like an ass. *"Sorry,"* he said, unprompted. *"No, I don't know what Jacoby's done now. Maybe his partner in crime isn't dead and decided to pay us a visit."*

The rest of the soldiers, tuned into their conversation, stilled. Jacoby's friend, Byers, showing up probably meant pain was imminent.

Once again, Formosa was reminded how much he'd failed, both for himself and for the other men here. He didn't know how much more any of them could take. He collected himself, putting on a brave face for the rest of them. *"I'm sure we'll be summoned to check things out soon,"* he said. *"Captain Barris?"*

There was a pause, and Formosa hoped the tank-bound captain was still conscious. He breathed a sigh of relief when the other man said, *"Right here."*

"Do you know anything about the ship landing here?"

Barris, bless him, didn't fuck around and get smart like the rest of Formosa's men sometimes did. *"I haven't heard anything, but I'm not in a position to investigate. I've been in this fucking tank for over twenty-four hours now."* There was a note of bitterness in his mental voice that hadn't been there before.

"I'm sorry," said Formosa, putting as much sincerity into the words he could. While Barris had a little more freedom with his movements and could talk, being trapped underwater, alone for those long stretches with only Jacoby for occasional company meant Formosa didn't envy him. At least the silenced cyborgs had each other. Nor was he envious of his relationship with Valenna. Well, not *terribly* envious.

"Not your fault," Barris said. *"But keep me posted on what's happening out there, would you? If Jacoby doesn't tell me first."*

Formosa promised to, then set back to work. As soon as he brushed away some snow from a generator, an unfamiliar voice blared into his head, its intensity making him jump.

"Omega-Three-Omega, this is the Gray Ghost. *I got your SOS."* The voice was female and held more self-assurance than Formosa ever had.

It also got the attention of everyone. All six men froze, waiting to hear more.

"I'm landing a few kilometers away from your installation. I coordinated a rescue with a newfound acquaintance," she continued. *"We're both looking for people on your base, but I'm on the lookout for Anders Barris."*

All of them exchanged glances with each other. *"Barris is here,"* said Formosa.

"I'm happy to hear that. Now, I need Garrett Jacoby's research, and I'm going to make sure no one can get to this place again after I've cleared you off-world. I'm planting some explosives before I bring in the cavalry. Do you think you can hold on for another few hours?"

Formosa closed his eyes, hardly daring to believe what he was hearing.

"Yes," he said. *"We've made it this long.* Gray Ghost, *thank you."*

Valenna was asleep when Jacoby burst into her barracks, turning on the harsh overhead illumination with a slap of his hand.

Her immediate thought was he'd discovered her message to Cressida and her feeble and low-tech attempts to cover her tracks. She sat bolt upright in bed, a part of her grateful that she was wearing pajamas. When she finally found her voice, all she could squeak out was, "What's going on?"

"Get up," Jacoby ordered.

"I will," she said, swinging her legs over the side of the bed. "But tell me what's happening."

"A ship's docked on our landing pad," he replied. He looked even more disheveled than when he was drinking, and she suspected he hadn't given himself a chance to recover from the hangover.

Hope flared in Valenna's heart, and she hoped it didn't show on her face. "Supplies?" she said lightly. Fully awake, she jumped out of bed and grabbed some clean clothes to change into when he finally took his leave.

"I haven't ordered supplies or personnel," Jacoby snapped.

He ran a hand through his hair, and she noticed he was still wearing the same clothes as he did during his binge.

"Maybe it's your friend," Valenna said.

"I considered that." Jacoby paced the floor. "But Colton would only leave his research facility if he absolutely had to."

"Maybe he absolutely had to," Valenna said. "That could be why he's gone off the grid."

She had to meet whoever had piloted that ship, if only to get a message to the outside world about what was happening on Omega-Three-Omega.

"It's possible," said Jacoby. "Whoever the captain is, he hasn't responded to my hails and he hasn't left."

"Does it have an ident?"

"Yes, but it isn't one I've authorized."

Valenna wanted to scream in frustration. *But what use would that be? How many people do you know who have ships?*

None. But there was one captain who she never wanted to see again unless it was to kill him. While she would love to hear that Janek Dalton had turned over a new leaf, she doubted it would happen. If Dalton had shown up here, that could only mean it was to lead the people to whom she owed money to her.

"I think it's the *Ensign*," Jacoby said, but the name meant nothing to Valenna. She was dying to ask about who her captain was, but didn't dare and give away what she'd done earlier.

"Okay," said Valenna. "What do you want me to do?"

"I've already ordered the grunts to deal with them," Jacoby said. "They'll be marching down to the landing pad about now, and the rest will continue to fix the fuel lines outside."

"And you need me for this?" Why did she have to babble when she was nervous?

"Just get dressed," Jacoby said. "We'll talk to these people, and you're the only other normal one here."

"But I'm not a soldier," Valenna said. "And I don't think I can pass for one."

"Just do it!" Jacoby glared at her.

"Can I have some privacy?"

He blinked like the concept was foreign to him. "Two minutes," he barked, then strode from the room.

"Five," she returned. "Let me brush my teeth at least."

As soon as Jacoby left her barracks, Valenna dressed and washed up, anxiety and cautious optimism warring within her. A ship's arrival so soon after she sent her SOS couldn't be a coincidence.

Her trip to Omega-Three-Omega had only taken a few hours. It had been a day since she sent that message to Cressida, plenty of time for a rescue to be planned.

If Cressida had arrived or sent someone. Valenna still wasn't sure her sister would be up for such a thing. Truthfully, she doubted she would do so in Cressida's place.

She fought back tears when she thought of Cressida and Lukas and what she'd done, blinking rapidly and swallowing the lump in her throat. Jacoby must suspect nothing about the ship's arrival other than what he already did.

Jacoby was waiting for her outside the barracks when she left, with two minutes to spare. He looked noticeably calmer. "They're bringing the captain here," he said. "He claims he has news about Byers."

Oh, no.

The ship hadn't brought rescue, only more misery for everyone here.

A tall, dark-haired man wearing a flight suit and heavy coat was escorted through the base's doors, flanked on either side by two soldiers. Clumsily embroidered ship's patches on his clothes read "Ensign." The doors cycled shut with a clang that echoed off the foyer's walls.

Valenna's knees threatened to give way beneath her, but she didn't fall. Instead, she eyed the stranger who regarded her with a friendly expression.

She'd seen him before, but where?

She racked her brain, looking for answers. Definitely not one of Dalton's associates, and he looked too healthy to be a darfin user. His attire was too shabby to belong to a darfin dealer, not that dealers did their own dirty work tracking down old debts.

So, who the hell was he?

She'd seen him in Center City, she was sure of it.

Her thoughts were interrupted when Jacoby stepped forward and spoke. "Who are you, and what's your purpose here?"

The stranger stuck out his hand. "Matthias Ericks, of the *Ensign*."

Ericks. The name was familiar.

She'd met him in her building, shortly after taking over Cressida's lease, months ago. He'd been looking for Lukas. Old military buddy, he'd said.

Hope flared in Valenna's heart, and she dearly hoped it wasn't misplaced.

The name of the man and the ship meant nothing to Jacoby. "You told my men you were here about Colton Byers," he said. "Is he with you?"

Matthias smiled. "No," he said. "I just have news about him I thought you needed to know about."

Jacoby cocked his head to the side impatient. Valenna expected him to tap his foot any second.

"He's dead," Matthias said bluntly, the smile never leaving his face. To the soldiers on either side of him, he said, "Do what you need to do."

Both of them sprang into action, one of them tackling Jacoby to the floor. The other turned to Valenna, his voice raspy from disuse. "You need to get out now."

Jacoby screamed and flailed, and Valenna heard something in him snap. She couldn't keep herself from shrieking at the sound.

Matthias grabbed her wrist. "We're leaving now."

"Did Cressida get my message?" she asked.

"She did, which is why I'm here, and we'll explain later. But we must leave this place, right now. It'll get worse before it gets better."

"There's someone I have to take with me," she said. "A lot of someones. But the one I need to take is still here, and he's trapped."

"Valenna," Matthias said, any trace of joviality evaporating from him. "We have to go, right now. We have to run back to my freighter. Cressida and Lukas are waiting there. These guys can take care of themselves. Let's *go.*"

The base doors opened again, and another pair of soldiers ran in. Matthias grabbed her wrist, and she had no choice but to follow, running into the cold, snowy night.

CHAPTER 13

VALENNA'S LUNGS burned as she ran, struggling to keep up with Matthias. She could barely breathe, let alone as him what the hell was going on.

A part of her wanted to turn back and rescue Anders. Another part of her couldn't turn away from the help Cressida arranged. She didn't know what to choose. She loved them both.

She thought she might collapse by the time they finally reached a small freighter, the word *Ensign* emblazoned on her hull in peeling paint. Its airlock door was open, and a rampway extended as she and Matthias reached it. A petite, dark-haired woman was at the top, features obscured by the light behind her, gesturing for them to come aboard. As the ramp met the snowy ground, the rumble of engines sounded in the air.

"Up!" Matthias yelled at her.

Valenna didn't dare disobey. Heart shattering into a million pieces, she ran up the ramp behind Matthias. As soon as she was on board the *Ensign*, the ramp was withdrawn and the door closed. She found herself in an airlock accessway, an EVA suit hanging on the wall near her.

The woman who ushered them aboard threw her arms around Matthias, who returned the hug. "You're okay," she said into his neck.

"I always am."

"I was worried." She disentangled herself and held out her hand to Valenna. "I'm Serena. You must be Valenna."

Valenna cautiously shook her head. "Hi. Thank you."

Footsteps sounded from nearby, and a familiar face popped into the airlock accessway.

"Cressy," Valenna breathed, hardly daring to believe the sight.

Before she could process what was happening, Cressida was enveloping Valenna in a hug, sniffles escaping her. "You just took off," Cressida whispered in her ear. "And I had no idea what happened to you until I got that message. Fucking Dalton wouldn't tell us anything." She pulled away enough to look Valenna square in the eye. "Why the fuck would you go to *Janek Dalton* for help?"

"He came to me," Valenna said. "And we have to go back to the base right now and save the rest of the guys. They're all cyborgs, too, and it's so horrible for them there." A sob broke her voice, and she nearly shouted her next words. "We can't leave them here!"

"We have to go now," Matthias said. "The other cyborgs can take care of themselves. But we need to skedaddle off this planet if we want to live."

"No!"

Valenna's outraged protest had everyone still. She spotted Lukas lingering in the corridor and pointed a finger at him. "You're a cyborg!" she said. "Can't you make everyone else here see why we have to save them?"

Lukas regarded her coolly for a moment. Then, in a quiet, clipped voice, he said, "They'll be fine. But we may not be if we don't take off now." He inclined his head to Matthias. "I suggest we return to the cockpit and take off. The *Gray Ghost* has already landed further away from the installation."

Matthias nodded. "Let's go."

Something monumental had happened.

"Anyone out there?" Anders asked on the cyborg-shared link. It had been quiet over the last couple of hours since Formosa told him rescue was on the way. But no one had bothered to update him.

What if his cyborg brothers were dead, finally destroyed by Jacoby? What about Valenna? Had the doctor discovered her call for help and punished her for it?

Anders paced the length of the tank, looking through the plastiglas from all angles, but no one else had entered the Oasis. Had he been totally forgotten?

He eyed the ladder that led to the tank's small deck. He remembered Valenna falling in after not listening to him about its dangers, then remembered what happened later.

His ocular cybernetics could discern that the ladder was still electrified, ribbons of charged energy surrounding it like a demonic fog, visible only to him. The charges on the rest of the tank, the ones that had burned Valenna, were weaker but still strong enough to cause him pain.

Formosa's voice finally sounded on their shared link. *"Sorry about that."*

"Glad to hear you," Anders said. *"I was getting worried."*

"Well, we have good news and bad news," Formosa said.

"Oh, God."

"The good news is help is here. The bad news is part of that help picked up Valenna an hour ago."

"What the fuck?" That had Anders's full attention. *"What do you mean, Valenna's been picked up? Who took her?"*

"A freighter came by and rescued her. Another ship's here and just broke down the doors. We're holding Jacoby but..."

Johnston interrupted Formosa. *"That fucker!"*

"What is it?" Anders demanded.

"Ralston and Danvers were holding Jacoby. The bastard did something to them and escaped. I just found their bodies. Fuck!"

Their communication was as close to telepathic as it could get, but Anders could still hear Johnston's raw grief, the sheer rage of what was done to all of them, the vengeance in his cybernetic heart for Ralston and Danvers just as clearly as if he'd used his vocal cords to speak the words.

That galvanized Anders into action. He eyed the tank wall, its forcefield not as strong as that on the ladder. The plastiglas extended about three meters up, the water two. Anders had never tried it before, but was it possible to scale the tank wall and drop off on dry ground on the other side?

It was a pity his underwater cybernetic enhancements hadn't included webbed hands with suction capability. Jacoby probably foresaw escape attempts from the tank, which would explain why the doctor hadn't made Anders into a total merman. And until now, Anders hadn't tried to escape, thanks to the sure knowledge of what would happen if he did. Until he attacked Jacoby in the lab the day of the power failure, he'd never fought back at all.

He had no reason to after Jacoby told him about Cecily's death. He'd had nothing to live for until he met Valenna and discovered there were others like him, even worse off.

It was worth a try. He couldn't let the rest of them fight Jacoby without at least trying to help.

He shook his head. He didn't have time to mope over his life and reasons to live or not. He toed off the boots that kept him anchored to the tank's floor, then held his breath and swam up to the surface.

It was always a little jarring when his body switched from breathing underwater to breathing real air. He'd stopped coughing after coming to the surface long ago, but there was always a chill in his cybernetic lungs that never fully went away, that he never truly got used to.

He made the short swim to the tank's wall and gingerly touched its surface. As expected, a shock zapped his fingertips, traveling up his arm, but it wasn't terrible. In fact, it was weaker than it should be. Maybe all the cyborg failsafes Jacoby installed weren't fully restored yet.

Or the power had been tampered with. That was more likely, but Formosa hadn't said anything to him about that. Either way, it was an unexpected blessing.

Now that he was at the surface, he could see he only had to scale about a meter and a half's worth of wall, maybe a little less. He brightened a little. He could handle the shocks for such a short time.

Bracing himself, he launched himself at the wall and gripped its smooth side as much as he could, hauling himself up to grip its edge. Now that he was actually doing it, the shocks definitely felt worse, increasing as he finally put both hands on the edge and lifted himself out of the water. "Shit," he said aloud, resisting the urge to let go and let himself drop. His cybernetics couldn't repair a fractured skull if he fell to the floor.

Finally, hands screaming in protest, he let himself dangle off the tank wall's edge, hoping he wasn't about to break something vital when he hit the floor. A final shock had him losing his grip, and he tumbled to the floor in an undignified, sodden heap.

He lay there for a few seconds, catching his breath, waiting for the stabbing pains in his palms and arms, legs and feet, to recede. Only then did he wiggle his body to make sure nothing was broken.

He didn't have time to run a full diagnostic on himself, so he got to his feet and rushed out of the Oasis, into the corridor beyond, and called for the rest of the cyborgs on their shared link. *"I'm out of the Oasis. Where are you guys?"*

He dripped water down the corridor as he looked for signs of life, wishing he had a weapon. It was a tense moment before Formosa answered. *"Trying to find Jacoby before we take off."*

"We?" Anders asked.

"There's a ship waiting to take us off-world," Formosa replied, a touch of uncharacteristic happiness in his voice. *"Her captain's here and took off to find Jacoby after he ran away from us. We split up to look for him."*

Anders only had more questions, but the most pressing issue for him right then was that they couldn't find Jacoby. "Where are you, you bastard?" he murmured.

He looked up at the emergency lights, dimmed since the power was restored. Jacoby's hidey-hole was somewhere close to the Oasis, according to Valenna.

She was gone. But she'd left a sign behind for them.

He tried to tamp down that pain, instead keeping an eye on the ceiling for an empty socket.

They had taken her away from him.

It was for the best. He'd even told her to run if she got the chance, and damn the rest of them. She hadn't signed up for what he and the rest of the grunts had. But that knowledge didn't lessen the ache in his heart.

When one loved something—or someone—he was supposed to set it free.

He wasn't as stealthy as he would have liked, nor as much as he was back when he was an active soldier, but he was as quiet as he could be in his wet sock feet, and he could only hope that his strength would be enough to overpower Jacoby. The ocular cybernetics' heat sensors scanned the corridors, looking for life forms nearby, but didn't pick up anything yet. Oh-Three-Oh didn't have so much as a mouse.

Except ... there was a faint heat signature nearby, through the corridor wall. Two of them. He might have missed them had he not been looking for it.

Anders looked up and saw an empty light socket.

Valenna had said the doorway was hidden, that it was camouflaged into the wall. Anders scanned the surface, looking for the seams that would indicate a door, and found them. They were faint, but now that he was focusing on them, distinct.

Jacoby had someone else in there with him, and if that was happening, it couldn't be good.

Summoning every iota of his strength, Anders kicked at the hidden door. It gave a little, and he kicked again. From inside Jacoby's hideaway, he heard the doctor grunt.

Anders put his shoulder into the door and pushed until it gave way and he stumbled into a small, darkened apartment.

Jacoby was tied to a chair with sonicuffs binding his hands and feet, and Anders didn't need his ocular enhancements to see he was sweating buckets. But that wasn't the most surprising detail of the bizarre scenario.

No, the sight that nearly stopped his cybernetic heart was the woman holding an illegal Melton weapon in her hand, pointed at Jacoby's head. A brainwave disruptor, gripped by someone Anders never expected to see again.

It took a few seconds for him to find his voice, and when he did, it sounded like Formosa, speaking with his vocal cords for the first time in years.

"*Cecily.*"

———————————

Valenna only consented to being strapped into a jumpseat in the *Ensign*'s galley-lounge combination when her rescuers threatened to confine her to a cabin until they reached Echo-7. Cressida was strapped in next to her, and on her other side was Serena, who was Matthias's partner.

She now fully understood why Cressida and Lukas were so angry with her, knew how it felt.

She waited until they'd cleared Oh-Three-Oh's atmosphere and the grind of the *Ensign*'s heavy air engines ceased before speaking. "Okay," she said. "Why didn't you wait for the rest of the people there?"

Serena and Cressida exchanged glances, and Serena was the one who spoke. Valenna guessed that they figured she was less likely to bite off her head. "There was another rescue mission coinciding with ours," Serena replied. "When Cressida got your message, she reached out to us because Matthias has this ship. He's an independent freighter and works this part of the Zone a lot."

"I still don't understand what the deal is with the other ship and why you left everyone there," she snapped. Cressida put a hand on her arm in a gesture that should have been reassuring, but just further pissed off Valenna.

"Cressida got your message and contacted us right away for help," Serena said patiently. "When I did some quick research into the facility here, I found out your message was also picked up by someone else who was also trying to conduct a rescue mission. We got in touch and coordinated things so we could take the base by surprise. The *Gray Ghost*'s captain told us in advance that she was going to be using a lot more force than we were, so we had to get you out of there as soon as possible. She likes explosives."

Valenna tried to wrap her head around all of this new information. "So, the other guys are being rescued," she said.

Serena nodded. "By someone who has the equipment and

experience to pull off that kind of extraction. She's non-military and..." Her expression shuttered. "Terrifying, if I'm going to be honest. I'd rather not get on her bad side."

"Where is she taking them?"

"That's not our concern," Cressida said gently. "The *Gray Ghost*'s captain felt it wasn't prudent for us to have too much information for everyone's safety."

"God damn it." Tears pricked at Valenna's eyes. "You're saying I'm never going to see Anders again."

Cressida and Serena exchanged glances. "He's the cyborg you're friends with?"

"If by 'friends' you mean what you and Lukas are, yeah, then friends," Valenna said bitterly. "You know, I get it now. I get why you two hated me so much for getting you off Haven."

"Val, neither of us..."

"Oh, fuck off," said Valenna, then immediately regretted it. She'd been rescued without being turned into a cyborg or forced into pregnancy. Cressida came through for her. She should be grateful for that. She turned teary eyes to her sister. "Look, I'm sorry. Just angry and hurting."

It wasn't a large freighter. She didn't know where she could go to be alone for a bit.

And there was one more question she needed answered. "Do either of you know of a Byers? Works in cybernetics? Jacoby was having fits when he stopped communicating with him, and he's convinced he's dead. I guess they're friends."

Cressida blanched. Serena smiled.

"Oh, he's dead," Serena said. "Very dead. I killed him myself."

CHAPTER 14

AS ANDERS WATCHED HIS SISTER—BACK from the dead, a harder look to her than he remembered—he thought he might actually be back in the Oasis, at the bottom of the tank, passed out.

But as much as it made more sense for him to be dreaming, his enhanced body told him differently. Jacoby was really bound to the chair, and it was really Cecily aiming a brainwave disruptor at him, its indicator light glowing red, set to kill.

"Cecily," he said, and stepped forward.

Without dropping her weapon, she smiled, but there was something feral about it that hadn't been there before. "Hi, big brother."

All he could think to ask was, "What are you doing here?"

She rolled her eyes. "What do you think I'm doing? Saving your ass. I've been looking for you for years." She adjusted her grip on the Melton and looked back at Jacoby. "This rescue went a lot easier than I thought it would, but since you killed a couple of Anders's brothers-in-arms, I'm not going to bother with turning you in to the authorities."

With that pronouncement, she pressed the weapon's trigger. A beam of bright blue light flowed from it, directly into Jacoby's temple. Anders registered the sizzling sound of cooked flesh, a noise and odor that nearly had him heaving as Jacoby slumped forward in his seat, a blackened ring on his head where the laser hit. Blood pooled at the strike sight, barely hiding exposed brain matter.

"What the fuck?" Anders yelled.

"I would've thought you'd be happy about that," Cecily said. "The man who manipulated you into this—" She gestured at him, still soaking wet—"Is now dead. You're free." She holstered her weapon.

"What happened to you?" Anders asked.

"Do you mean my heart or...?" She let the question fade away, then looked at Jacoby's corpse.

"Both." The Cecily he'd grown up with was gentle, the last person who would ever hurt someone.

"It's been four years," she said. "We'll get off this rock and then I'll tell you all about it, okay? I still have to find some stuff before we leave and blow up this place." She turned away and started poking through a desk Anders hadn't noticed until now. "He had blueprints and schematics I need to take back with me, and we'll need them anyway for the rest of you guys." She picked up a thincomp and tucked it under her arm. "Can you connect with the other cyborgs?"

"How did you know about that? And what do you mean, 'blow up this place'?"

"I know about your secret link. I connected with Jason on it when I landed. Can you use that or an internal comm system to get them over here? The sooner we find all of Jacoby's notes, the sooner we can leave." She looked up from the desk, frustration across her fine-boned features. "And obviously, this place needs to explode. There can't be any evidence left of its existence in case someone else takes it upon himself to create more cyborgs. Officially, it's been abandoned by the military."

"Jason? Who's Jason?"

She sighed. "The tall one. Can you just get them in here? This place is connected to the base's sickbay, so we should be able to do a sweep quickly."

"It connects to the lab? How do you know that?"

"I was able to get a blueprint before I arrived," she said. "It wasn't easy, but I got it." She strode through the room, then turned around when Anders didn't immediately follow. "Well, come on."

Anders did so, but it took effort to move his feet. He was still too shocked at everything that had happened so quickly that it took a few tries to link himself into the cyborgs' connection.

Formosa replied. *"Where are you?"*

"Jacoby's dead," Anders said. *"Come to the lab. I guess you talked to my sister, or was it one of the other guys?"*

Formosa was quiet. *"That was your sister?"*

"I take it your first name is Jason?"

"It is. What the fuck is your sister doing here? She's the Gray Ghost's *captain? Don't get me wrong, I'm glad she's here, but this situation keeps getting more bizarre. You're* sure *Jacoby's dead?"*

"I saw Cecily use a brainwave disruptor on him and then watched his brains leak out of his head, so yeah, I'm pretty sure he's dead."

"Wow. All right. I'll find the others, and we'll get to the lab."

Anders noted the modest space Jacoby had been living in, its lack of personal touches except a couple of liquor bottles in a corner. The bedroom area had an open doorway that led into the lab where Cecily was already poking through drawers and shelves.

He walked into it, then looked back at the bedroom. The door was hidden behind a cabinet. "What the hell," he said quietly.

The surviving soldiers walked in through the doorway Anders was already familiar with, the one that led in from the Oasis. Formosa was in front, dark half-circles under his eyes. He looked like hell. All of them did.

Cecily looked up at their arrival. "I deactivated Jacoby's control over your voice boxes," she said. "It was the first thing I did with my Melton."

"Where did you get that?" Anders asked.

Both she and Formosa gave him a look that said it didn't matter. The other cyborgs started jerking open drawers and cabinets, looking for data devices. "I acquired it," Cecily said, not that it was an answer. "It's useful when it comes to making people talk, and that's what I did. He had a modified minicomp in his pocket that he was perfectly happy to hand over to me after I zapped him to do so, and I have that here." She patted her own pocket. "Now, I just have to find some stuff here before we go."

The only reason Anders wanted to get away from Oh-Three-Oh was so he could catch up with Valenna, so he didn't protest Cecily's insistence on leaving. Still, he was curious. "Why is this so important?" he asked. "Can't we just go and forget about this place?"

Cecily grabbed a few other things and shoved them in a bag she pulled out from her back pocket. "I just need to get this stuff."

"You still haven't told me how and why you're alive."

"God!" She slammed the bag on top of a bed. "I think it would be obvious, but I found someone who could get me a heart!"

Awful realization at her words' implication hit him. "And you're in debt to whoever gave it to you." Shades of Valenna. How was he going to get Cecily out of this mess?

"No," she said, so sharply, everyone looked at her. "I'm not in debt. I *cho*se this life, and you'll have to be okay with that. We're all on borrowed time before my bombs detonate, so we need to leave."

"Where did Valenna go?"

Formosa cleared his throat, then croaked, "Are you serious?"

"Is she the one the *Ensign* was looking for? Probably back to Echo-7. You can find her later." She looked around the lab. "Any luck? I have a minicomp, two thincomps, and some smaller data drives."

Johnston cleared his throat, tried to speak, then gave up. He held up a data drive and pointed at the main diagnostic console.

"Copy everything you can, even if it's encrypted," Cecily said. "I'll deal with that later."

"What do you mean?" Anders asked. "Are you turning us over to someone worse than Jacoby?" He remembered the doctor's colleague. "Byers? Is that it?"

"Byers is dead. I found that out the hard way." She made a face and shuddered. "He was long dead by the time I tracked down his moon compound."

That news heartened Anders. "But where are you planning on taking us?"

"Across the border. You know the war's over, right?"

Anders nodded. "That was one of the first things Valenna told me."

"Well, we can go over the border without a visa or work permit, at least for now. I'm sure they'll put a stop to it since life isn't as shitty over there and Zone citizens are moving in droves, but we'll worry about that when the time comes." She looked at Johnston, who was copying the diagnostic comp's data. "How's everything going over there?"

Johnston gave her a thumbs-up.

"Good. I think this will be all. Do any of you have personal effects you want to take with you?" To Anders, she said, "Do you want to get changed?"

He did come to think of it. "Yeah."

"Do that, come back here, and then we'll leave," she said. "I know you have questions."

Despite Valenna's protests, Cressida insisted she return to the apartment she shared with Lukas when they returned to Echo-7. Even though she didn't want to, she had to admit it made sense. It was nearly ten in the evening when the *Ensign* left them at a public dock near their apartment block, and another twenty minutes before they made it to their home.

Her old apartment would have been rented to someone else since she vacated it, and she didn't have any possessions for the time being. At least she wasn't broke: Serena had done something to Jacoby's accounts and transferred her more than enough of her promised wages. Valenna could easily replace her meager wardrobe and thincomp. She had enough to start over, away from Echo-7, like she'd wanted in the first place.

She'd vowed never to return here again, and it rankled her that not only did she have to, but she would also be spending the next few days with her sister and her sister's boyfriend who hated her. "I can stay at a hotel," she said for what felt like the hundredth time since she arrived at their apartment. Cressida shoved a glass of water in her hand, like that was going to make everything okay again.

"At least stay here for the night," said Cressida. "I'm just glad you're all right." She took a seat next to Valenna on the couch where Valenna would be sleeping.

"You were worried I'd relapsed," Valenna said.

The look on Cressida's face told her she was right. "That's part of your safety," she said. "I had all these awful scenarios running through my head when I couldn't get in touch with you and your apartment's lock was changed. You've been really good about communication since you got out of rehab. I liked that."

"I really tried this time," Valenna said, hating the tears that pricked at the backs of her eyes.

"I know you did, and this time it worked," Cressida said gently. "I want you to do well and be happy. I love you."

"I love you too, but I can't stay in Center City," Valenna said. "I need to leave." She sniffled. "I have enough now to do that. I'm probably going to go over the border after I pay off the rest of my debt." She'd make arrangements to have what she owed put into escrow and then let Dalton take care of it. The bounty hunter was a piece of shit, but he wouldn't hesitate to turn over indebted funds to the kinds of people Valenna used to associate with.

"No darfin or dealers in the Brava System," she added. "At least none that I know." She looked around the apartment, decorated with dozens of holos Cressida had taken over the years, and its brightly colored furniture. Even though it was a run-of-the-mill apartment for Center City, Cressida and Lukas had managed to make it into a cheerful home.

"I know," Cressida said. "I get it. But please remember you'll always have a home with us."

Valenna snorted at that and sneaked a glance at Lukas.

"It's true," he said quietly. "You tried to save those cyborgs. You didn't have to do that."

"Why didn't you?" she demanded.

"Because the *Ensign* doesn't have the capacity to house that number of people, and someone else was already on the way to do that," Lukas said. "The *Gray Ghost*'s captain has been looking for Anders Barris for some time. She managed to trace me, since I'm the only official cyborg in existence, right as we were trying to find you. If I believed in a deity, I'd think it was divine intervention. Wherever they are, your cyborg friends are safe."

"I need to get back to them," Valenna said. "I need to get back to Anders."

"I don't know how to do that," Lukas said. "If you ask Serena, she may be able to do so, but even she's a little scared of the *Gray Ghost*'s captain."

"Serena killed that Byers guy." Valenna still couldn't believe that.

"A fitting punishment for the man who murdered her parents for her and turned her into a more sophisticated cyborg than I'll ever be," Lukas said.

Valenna had sulked for the remainder of the trip back to Echo-7, and after Serena admitting to killing a guy, she hadn't wanted to talk to her that much. The news about her being a cyborg was a surprise. "What?"

"Her cybernetic functions have been disabled to improve her quality of life," Lukas said, as if that made any difference to her being a cyborg. Valenna could hardly believe it. Serena didn't have any visible ports or anything that indicated she was enhanced.

She recalled Jacoby's wish for a baby to experiment on, how he'd told her that Byers acquired a kid of his own. Serena must have been that kid.

"And the man she killed deserved it," Lukas continued. "I'm not one for violence anymore, but Colton Byers was vile. So was Garrett Jacoby, now that we know what happened." His gaze fixed on Valenna, but for the first time, his look didn't seem resentful. "You did your best back there."

"I don't even know if Anders is okay," Valenna whispered. "That's what kills me."

She didn't get a chance to tell him she loved him or kiss him goodbye. She'd let herself be taken away. She should have fought harder.

"I'm sure he'll be okay," Lukas said, voice uncharacteristically soft. "I made it on my own for years on Haven. Cyborgs are nothing if not resourceful. That's what we're designed to be."

Valenna hated to think of Anders as a thing, but she could only nod. At least Lukas had warmed up to her a little. This was the first time she hadn't felt completely unwelcome in his presence.

"I think I'd like to go to bed now," she said.

"Me, too," said Cressida, standing up. "It's been a very long day for all of us. Lukas?"

Lukas nodded, and they went to their bedroom off the living area, leaving Valenna alone.

Frantic knocking at the apartment door had Valenna sitting upright, heart pounding, and mouth dry. Who the hell could that be? Was it the dealer who wanted a holo of her with blackened eyes?

It would never fucking end while she stayed in the Zone. The threat of someone coming after her or her sister would always persist as long as people knew she was in Center City.

She got up from the couch and crossed the room to the apartment door, checking the apartment's visualizer feed next to the jamb.

She thought she might be hallucinating when she saw who was on the other side, but she still opened the door.

Anders, none the worse for wear, stood before her.

She blurted out the first words that came to mind. "Do you know what time it is?" It was either that or she would start crying.

"Yeah, it's nearly four in the morning," he replied. "And I came to ask you to come to the Brava System with me."

"Who's there?" Lukas's voice bellowed through the apartment, making Valenna jump. She turned around to see him in the bedroom's doorway, Cressida behind him.

"It's Anders," Valenna said, grabbing his hand. "Anders, this is my sister, Cressida Merchant, and her partner, Lukas Best."

Anders inclined his head to them, who relaxed a little after Valenna's introduction. "I've heard a lot about both of you."

"Likewise," said Lukas.

To Valenna, Anders said, "Do you want to go?"

"Go where?" said Cressida, pushing past Lukas. "Val, what's he talking about?"

"That new start," Valenna whispered, looking up at him. "What happened to everyone else?"

"We lost Danvers and Ralston," Anders said, and with that statement, Valenna felt a corresponding pain in her heart. "Jacoby got to them before he was neutralized."

"You killed Jacoby?"

"No," he replied. "My sister did."

"Cecily?" Valenna again thought this might be a hallucination. "I thought she was dead!"

"She isn't, and it's a very long story. So long, she still hasn't told me all of it. She found out where your sister lives, guessed you'd be here, and she was right." He grabbed Valenna's hands in his own, so warm and familiar. "Do you want to go?"

"Now?"

He nodded. "Cecily's ship's waiting for us at a spaceport near here."

Valenna looked back at Cressida and Lukas. Cressida gave her a tiny nod.

"Yes."

It didn't take long for Valenna to dress, and through tears, say goodbye to Cressida and Lukas. This day had to come; it had just arrived a little sooner than Valenna anticipated.

Hand in hand, she and Anders left the apartment block and caught a waiting private auto-shuttle cab to take them to the spaceport where his sister's ship waited. "I really tried to save you back there," she said.

"I know. I also told you to take the first chance you got to escape," he reminded her. "I'm glad you got away."

"I was angry that I didn't get a chance to tell you I love you," said Valenna. The auto-shuttle dipped a little, moving Valenna a little closer to Anders, then righted its course.

"I didn't get a chance to kiss you hello back there, either," said Anders.

His lips pressed against hers, tongue demanding entrance. Valenna moaned and wrapped her hands around his neck, wishing they had more time to spend alone together than the four minutes the auto-shuttle said they had. He pulled away from enough to say, "And I love you, too."

Valenna settled against him, a feeling of contentment and rightness spreading through her for the first time in her life. She was meant to be with him, was meant to start her life over in a new system with him.

The shuttle descended over the spaceport, warning lights flashing for anyone below it. Valenna saw a boxy ship about ten meters away, the only one this early in the morning, and pointed at it. Anders nodded. "That's the *Gray Ghost*. Cecily's her captain."

The auto-shuttle's doors squeaked open, and Anders helped her out of the vehicle. "Ready?" he asked.

Valenna smiled and nodded, and they walked to the waiting ship.

Jessica Marting is a sci-fi and paranormal romance author, art enthusiast (not quite an artist, despite all that time in art school), an avid reader, and makeup collector. She lives in Toronto.

Sign up for her newsletter at jessicamarting.com/newsletter for pre-order alerts, sales, freebies, and more.

ALSO BY JESSICA MARTING

Castaways

Demon's Favor

Ingram Content Group UK Ltd.
Milton Keynes UK
UKHW010723200423
420491UK00004B/236